the celtic fan

by
Deanndra Hall

The Celtic Fan
Copyright © 2014 Deanndra Hall
Print Edition

Celtic Muse Publishing, LLC
P.O. Box 3722
Paducah, KY 42002-3722

This book is a work of fiction.

Names of characters, places, and events are the construction of the author, except those locations that are well-known and of general knowledge, and all are used fictitiously. Any resemblance to persons living or dead is coincidental, and great care was taken to design places, locations, or businesses that fit into the regional landscape without actual identification; as such, resemblance to actual places, locations, or businesses is coincidental. Any mention of a branded item, artistic work, or well-known business establishment is used for authenticity in the work of fiction and was chosen by the author because of personal preference, its high quality, or the authenticity it lends to the work of fiction; the author has received no remuneration, either monetary or in-kind, for use of said product names, artistic work, or business establishments, and mention is not intended as advertising, nor does it constitute an endorsement. The author is solely responsible for content.

Cover design 2014, M.D. Halliman
Tattoo design 2014, Carrie Jones, used by permission of the artist.
Formatted by BB eBooks

Disclaimer:

This work contains sexually suggestive material and depictions of sexual acts that some individuals might deem unsuitable for those 13 years of age or under. Discretion is advised.

More titles from this author:

Love Under Construction Series

The Groundbreaking – Summer 2013

The Groundbreaking is a preview of the main characters contained in all of the Love Under Construction series novels. Not intended as a work of erotic fiction, it is simply a way for the reader to get to know and love each character by discovering their backgrounds. This series contains graphic situations that are unsuitable for readers under 18 years of age.

Laying a Foundation (Book 1) – Fall 2013

Sometimes death robs us of the life we thought we'd have; sometimes a relationship that just won't die can be almost as bad. And sometimes the universe aligns to take care of everything. When you've spent years alone, regardless the circumstances, getting back out there can be hard. But when you've finally opened up to love and it looks like you might lose it all, can love be enough to see you through?

Tearing Down Walls (Book 2) – Fall 2013

Secrets – they can do more damage than the truth. Secrets have kept two people from realizing their full potential, but even worse, have kept them from forming lasting relationships and finding the love and acceptance they both desperately need. Can they finally let go of those secrets in time to find love – and maybe even to stay alive?

Renovating a Heart (Book 3) – Spring 2014

Can a person's past really be so bad that they can never recover from it? Sometimes it seems that way. One man hides the truth of a horrific loss in his teen years; one woman hides the truth of a broken, scarred life that took a wrong turn in her teens. Can they be honest with each other, or even with themselves, about their feelings? And will they be able to go that distance before one of them is lost forever?

Planning an Addition (Book 4) – Fall 2014

When you think you're set for life and that life gets yanked out from under you, starting over is hard. One woman who's starting over finds herself in love with two men who've started over too, and she's forced to choose. Or is she? And when one of them is threatened by their past, everyone has choices to make. Can they make the right ones in time to save a life?

The Harper's Cove Series

Beginning with the flagship volume, *Karen and Brett at 326 Harper's Cove*, find out exactly what the neighbors of Harper's Cove are up to when they go inside and close their doors. According to Gloria, the drunken busy-body of the cove, they're all up to something perverse, and she's determined to find out their secrets. As she sneaks, peeks, pokes, and prods, her long-suffering husband, Russell, begs her to leave all of their nice neighbors alone. But could Gloria be right?

The Harper's Cove series books are fast, fun, nasty little reads priced just right to provide a quick, naughty romp. See if the neighbors of Harper's Cove shock you just enough to find out what the occupants of the next address will do! This series is somewhere between erotic romance and erotica and is not suitable for readers under the age of 18 years.

Karen and Brett at 326 Harper's Cove

Gloria wants more than anything to be invited to one of Karen and Brett Reynolds' parties, and she's very vocal about it. Karen and Brett, however, know full well that if Gloria were ever invited to one of their parties, she would be in a hurry to leave, and in an even bigger hurry to let everyone know they are the scourge of the neighborhood. Every Saturday night, Karen and Brett keep their secrets – all twelve of them.

Donna and Connor at 228 Harper's Cove

Those nice people at 228, the Millicans? They're religious counselors, trying to help lovely couples who are having marital problems. Problem is, they're not counseling; training, maybe, but not counseling. But no matter what Donna says, Gloria still thinks the truck that delivered large crates to the Millicans' house in the wee hours of the morning, two weeks after they'd moved in, was pretty suspicious. Donna says it was exercise equipment that the moving company had lost, but Gloria's not so sure. Could it be that they're not as they appear?

Becca and Greg at 314 Harper's Cove

Even though they're quiet and stay to themselves, Becca and Greg Henderson seem pretty nice and average. They don't go out much or have many people over, except for that one couple who are probably relatives. But when that half-sister of Becca's moves in, it all seems a little fishy; she gets around pretty well for a person recovering from cancer. And where was Becca going all decked out in that weird outfit? The Hendersons are tight-lipped, but Gloria hopes she can eventually get to the bottom of things. If she does, she'll get the biggest surprise of her life.

And we're just getting started!

A word from the author . . .

This novel is nothing short of a miracle.

In the summer of 2000, my then-teenage daughter took a trip to Europe with a high school group. She hadn't been gone twenty-four hours before I had an idea. I'd been writing for years, but I'd never been able to work up the nerve to write a book. So I set out to do just that.

I began writing and, as I did, the words began to pour out of my fingertips. They were so passionate and lovely that I couldn't stop. I wrote in a frenzy because I knew that once my daughter walked back into the house, I'd go back into "full-time mom mode" and that would be it – it would never be finished.

I wrote. I wrote for three nights and four days. Without sleeping. Barely eating. Only occasionally getting up to go to the bathroom or stretch. Writing was all I did. And I finished it the day before she was set to return. Late that evening, after a nap, I opened the file and read through it. I'd assumed that, considering the way in which it was put down, it would be a four door, brass-plated disaster, and I was shocked to find that it was both clear and beautiful. Then I closed the file, caught up all of the things I was supposed to do while she was gone, picked her up from the airport, and never looked at it again.

In the next five years I devoted an enormous amount of time to writing, but I never went back to the book.

What I did do was amass a huge number of short stories and poems, and started another book which, for the record, is somewhere between two-thirds and three-quarters complete (guess you know what one of my next projects will be!). But I never looked at the first book again.

Time passed. I'd stored the files on three and one-half inch floppies. Somewhere along the line, I had one of those hideous Zip drives, and they got moved around to those cartridges too.

Several years and three computers later, to my horror, I found that the files were gone. I looked everywhere, scoured old floppy disks, searched through old hard drives. Nothing. They had vanished, lost in the technological shuffle.

Oddly enough, in mid-October 2013, over thirteen years after I'd first written this book, I was telling my partner about it. I'd never even mentioned it to him before, and after I explained the plot, I lamented, "It was really, really good. I wish I still had it."

And then, on Halloween night – Samhain to me – he was recounting his trip to our ancient county courthouse that day and telling me about a clock crashing down from the wall, almost hitting a lady passing by. He said one of the security guards commented, "Yeah, we've had lots of poltergeist activity today." We laughed about it.

But as I went to bed, I had a sudden thought: I'd bought a brand-new external hard drive, and it occurred to me that, although I backed up my files every night, I'd never checked to see if they really were backed up. I went back to my computer to check and found that they had not transferred, and my heart froze. I had to back them up. What if lightning struck? I'd lose everything I'd been working on, including several completed manuscripts. So I manually copied files, then opened the external hard drive to check and see if they were really there. I went to the search bar and typed in "writing."

Up popped dozens of files, things I couldn't identify. I stared at them in disgust, wondering what junk they could possibly be and where they could've possibly come from. I opened one that seemed particularly odd, and gasped.

There they were. The book; four books, in fact. All of the short stories. All of the poetry. Everything I'd wondered about, looked for, lost – all on a brand-new external hard drive.

To this very moment, I still have no clue how they got there. No one was more surprised than I, and I began to cry to the extent that my partner came to see what was wrong. I couldn't believe it. It didn't make sense, and yet there they were. I made note of where they were located, closed the files, shut down the computer for the night, and went to bed, barely able to sleep.

It was with shaking hands and a racing heart that I opened the file for *The Celtic Fan* the next morning and had the distinct, unimaginable joy of seeing these words intact and as beautiful as they were initially, a full thirteen years since their original writing. As I surveyed the manuscript, I realized that there was very little left to do to it to make it ready for publication. It was, and continues to be, the cleanest, tightest manuscript I never edited. Seriously. I'm not kidding.

As I write this, I'm waiting for some artwork, and then the photo shoot for the cover art will take place. I still find it hard to believe that a work I thought was lost forever will in just a few short weeks be out there to be enjoyed by anyone who wishes to read a story, two actually, that will grip their heart to the last sentence.

So, to my daughter, whose trip made this possible (without her knowledge, of course), and to my partner, who shared my joy and read the manuscript with wonder, I love you both; and to Steve, Diana, Claire, and Bill, I love you and can barely wait to share your story with the world.

And I think my next vacation will be to Ebbs Mill!

Love and happy reading,
Deanndra

P.S. From this point forward, the voice you hear will be Steve's. He tells his story better than anyone else could.

Visit me at: www.deanndrahall.com

Connect with me on my Substance B page:
substance-b.com/DeanndraHall.html

Contact me at: DeanndraHall@gmail.com

Join me on Facebook at: facebook.com/deanndra.hall

Catch me on Twitter at: twitter.com/DeanndraHall

Find me blogging at: deanndrahall.blogspot.com

Write to me at:
P.O. Box 3722, Paducah, KY 42002-3722

Support your Indie authors!

Independent (Indie) authors are not a new phenomenon, but they are a hard-working one. As Indie authors, we write our books, have trouble finding anyone to beta read them for us, seldom have money to hire an editor, struggle with our cover art, find it nearly impossible to get a reviewer to even glance at our books, and do all of our own publicity, promotion, and marketing. This is not something that we do until we find someone to offer us a contract – this is a conscious decision we've made to do for ourselves that which we'd have to do regardless (especially promotion, which publishers rarely do anyway). We do it so big publishing doesn't take our money and give us nothing in return. We do it because we do not want to give up rights to something on which we've worked so hard. And we do it because we want to offer you a convenient, quality product for an excellent price.

Indie authors try to bring their readers something fresh, fun, and different. Please help your Indie authors:

   – Buy our books! That makes it possible for us to continue to produce them;

   – If you like them, please go back to the retailer from which you bought them and review them for us. That helps us more than you could know;

– If you like them, please tell your friends, relatives, nail tech, lawn care guy, anyone you can find, about our books. Recommend them, please;

– If you're in a book circle, always contact an Indie author to see if you can get free or discounted books to use in your circle. Many would love to help you out;

– If you see our books being pirated, please let us know. We worked weekends, holidays, and through vacations (if we even get one) to put these books out, so please report it if you see them being stolen.

More than anything else, we hope you enjoy our books and, if you do, please contact us in whatever manner we've provided as it suits you. Visit our blogs and websites, friend our Facebook sites, and follow us on Twitter. We'd love to get to know you!

INTRODUCTION

Writing is all I've ever done; it's all I'll ever do. It's what I trained to do, what I allowed myself to be educated to do, and what I've done ever since I can remember. It can be the easiest thing in the world or the hardest. Journalism is hard work. But journalism didn't prepare me for this.

This was the hardest. When I began trying to put this story into words, I met my match for the first time in my life. How do you pen down emotions, intuitions, nuances? What's the key to writing down the sky, or the water, or the look of the breeze in the hair of a fine, handsome woman? That was my challenge, my agony, my pleasure. What transpires within these pages was nothing short of a miracle to me. I don't expect it to affect you so profoundly – that's just not possible. Like the old saying goes, "You just had to be there."

As a means of explanation and, hopefully, inspiration, I have included at the end of each chapter a portion of the original work that birthed this whole lovely adventure. Please note that I do indeed have the author's permission, even encouragement, to use these excerpts. Traveling through these pages, you will eventually gain a deep appreciation for this inclusion. Of that I'm sure.

So please read on. This is without a doubt my finest piece of work ever. It would not exist, however, without the most transcendent of inspirations, and it is to her that I dedicate this book.

S.J.R.

chapter 1

The office had been crazy all day, so I was more than a little annoyed that the phone at home was ringing as I struggled through the door. I didn't even take time to turn on the light before I answered it. It was Russ, it was the end of March, and it was a little past the time of year for "The Call." Didn't matter that he was a little late. I knew it would come.

"Hey, man, what's up?" was the usual greeting, and this time was no different. "About ready for the inevitable?"

"Of course. Little slow this year, huh?" I quipped, pinching the receiver between ear and shoulder, flipping on the light and trying to unload my briefcase, jacket, and all the other junk I'd dragged in from the car.

"Well, I hadn't had my usual blinding flash of insight until today. But I've got it now, an epiphany, sheer genius. Dinner tomorrow night, about seven, at the Italian restaurant at Lincoln Crossing?"

"Sure. Seven at Lincoln Crossing. Jim and Michael?"

"They're planning on it," he assured me. "By the way, read the book yet?"

My mind went blank. "What book?"

"You know, the one Michael loaned you. The Nick Roberts book," he chided.

That was a peculiar question. "How'd you know about that?"

"I asked him to loan it to you; good thing too. Better read it," he sing-songed. "Otherwise you won't know what we're talking about."

"When?"

"At dinner tomorrow night."

"I thought we were talking about the trip tomorrow night," I half stated, half asked, trying to get a better grip on the conversation.

"We are. See you tomorrow night." He hung up before I had a chance to ask anything else. I looked at the phone for a couple of seconds before I put it down. Strange conversation, but exactly what I'd come to expect from Russ.

Every spring we took these trips, had for at least fifteen years. And every summer Russ came up with something even more fantastic or knot-headed than before, most often being the latter rather than the former. There'd been the trip planned around the garden tours in Savannah, Georgia, and Natchez, Mississippi, because Russ insisted he'd found some guy along the way who made moonshine the old-fashioned way. And he wasn't kidding. Problem was, the ATF knew about the fellow too, and we almost got caught helping the "chef" draw off and bottle his brew. Have to admit, though, that until the bust it was a sweet, sweet trip.

Then there was the foray into the world of blue movies, when Russ discovered one of his coworkers had a brother who was a porn director and needed a crew to shoot a budget film. That had to go down as one of the best trips we've ever taken. The movie plot, if you could call it that, was about twenty-five babes trapped in an old monastery with a madman who used them as sex slaves. Only one man, the one who played their captor, was in the cast, and there were twenty-five hot chicks available, plus extras, so we had plenty of girls to do in our free time.

And thinking about being trapped reminds me of the worst trip ever. We visited a fabulous island resort which, as best I recall, Russ had described as a "fantasy land." I use the words "fabulous" and "resort" loosely. Island is the only part of the description that was accurate. No running water, dirt-floor huts, canned C-rations three meals a day. The local island women didn't quite match the reports we'd been given, either. Their combined tooth count was eight and a half, and they all weighed out at the extreme ends of the scale, either over three hundred pounds or barely seventy-five. Russ and Michael found themselves a couple of the local enterprising teenage girls with whom to play slumber party, but no way was I going to get involved in that. No foreign jails for this guy, no sir. After enough mosquito bites to play connect-the-dots for a couple of years, the blessed boat came and took us away from our tropical exile none too soon for me. Now, every time Russ mentions an island or the tropics, the other three of us run like hell.

It had been almost a year since the last delightful excursion and now it was time to discuss Russ's latest concept for an exciting break from reality, but I had to wonder what that book had to do with a trip. I'd intentionally put off reading the thing. It was the last piece of crying-in-your-beer, broken-hearted trash I'd want to look at. Every review I'd read about it compared it to *The Bridges of Madison County*, which I'd personally thought was the biggest piece of crap to come down the pike in a long time. What kind of guy would like reading stuff like that? But everyone kept raving about *The Celtic Fan*, and then Michael loaned it to me. "Read it," he'd said. "I'll just loan it to you. You won't even have to buy it. But you'll miss out if you don't read it."

"Did you really read it?" I'd quizzed, grinning and squinting at Mr. Macho from the corner of my eye.

"Yes, Steve," he'd smiled. "I really did read it. Really. And it's unlike anything else I've ever read. You've got to read it. You'll see. I know you think you won't like it, but you will, trust me. You'll see what all the hype's about."

My imagination ran wild as I thought about his repetitious insistence – *you'll see, you'll see, you'll see*. Putting away the things I brought in from the car, I opened the refrigerator door. There were five more beers glittering under the bare bulb's light. The new case I'd picked up at the store fit in the cavernous interior with room to spare, a reminder that I should probably take the plunge and buy some food to go with the beer next time. Popping the top off one of the already-cold brews, I wandered across the room to the table in front of the picture window. The book was there, face down to keep the front cover from tempting me into betrayal of my resolve, and it was a beautiful cover at that. As I thumbed through it, I checked out the last few pages. It was only about two hundred and seventy-five pages long, just enough to read in a quiet evening. Mental inventory: four more beers. They would be enough to last until I'd finished reading.

Relaxing in the comfort of the recliner, elixir in hand, I dropped the book into my lap and turned on the overhead light. The beer bottle cast an amber shadow across the cover, making it hard to get a good look at the photo, so I moved the bottle back on the chairside table and held the bluish-green volume up to the light. The cover was dominated by a photo in a pale moss green and sepia tone, sort of yellowish against the darkness of the cover. It was a picture of a woman, mostly of her left arm, soft and feminine, with some kind of filter slightly blurring the shot in a way that left it dream-like and gentle. Taken from above and over the model's shoulder, the elbow was bent at a ninety-degree angle, the underside of the forearm exposed, and the hand tipped slightly downward, palm up, so that the veins and tendons were pronounced and vulnerable. It looked almost as though a hand would drop from the right side of the picture and slash a knife blade across the narrow, graceful wrist, almost as though the veins were being offered up, a sort of sacrificial gesture. On the wrist was a tiny tattoo, fan-shaped and tan against the sepia-toned flesh, contrasting with the mossy green color of the book jacket. There was a design inside the borders of the tattoo, but it was impossible to make out a pattern. Guessing from the title, I assumed the contents of the diminutive border were somehow Celtic in nature, maybe small knots or something, but I really couldn't tell. And in the model's hand was a ring of some sort, just a simple band as it appeared. Although the author's name, Nick Roberts, was a typical Times New Roman-looking thing, the title was done in a decidedly Celtic-style font, looking somewhat like letters carved on a tombstone. In those letters, that name, was the cause of all the fuss over the book.

Seems no one knew Nick Roberts. No one knew who he was, where he was, or from whence he came. He didn't do interviews, didn't answer questions through his publisher or agent, didn't call in to radio talk shows, didn't appear on late-night television. As a matter of fact, no one had ever seen him, as I understood it. That was one of the reasons the book became so popular. Want to sell a million books? Be elusive, mysterious. Literature buffs value that in a writer, though I don't have a clue why that's considered a positive character trait. Maybe it's because all writers are supposedly crazy. I guess that means all readers have to be a little off the beam to understand the writers, right? Not much comfort to a newspaper man like myself.

I opened the front of the book and noticed absolutely no sound, no cracking of glue or sticky pages like most of the books I'd borrowed from friends. This one was well worn and fell open easily, lying flat in my lap, its welcoming arms beckoning me to devour it. I decided to start by reading through the introduction, which was usually helpful in gaining an understanding of the author. This intro didn't help at all, dealing more with the background of the setting and the curiosities of the story. It didn't really tell one single thing about the author, nothing. Zip. But it was good, as introductions go.

The introduction flew past, and I began to delve into the first chapter. That's all I remember about the beginning. It was gone in a flash, and I was drawn into the story, completely immersed, the words washing over me. Time stood still. The world around me evaporated. Bill and Claire, the principal characters, became as real as anyone I'd ever known, their hearts beating almost audibly from the pages. And something unbelievable happened.

I never got up to get another beer.

They drew closer and he shifted, squirmed somewhat, trying in vain to hide the crutches. Perhaps they wouldn't notice in the dim light escaping from the tavern window that he wasn't whole, that he was flawed and uneven.

"Hey, beautiful!" Johnny grinned, blocking the redhead's path. Seemingly annoyed, she answered, "Hey yourself." But Bill wasn't looking at the blond. He was looking at her friend.

Ivory skin glowed in the beams falling through the smoky glass. Even the lack of illumination couldn't hide the deep auburn streaks in her chestnut hair or the sparkle in her dark eyes. She smiled shyly, peering out at him from behind the wisps of hair falling down her forehead. For a brief moment the crutches didn't matter, nor did the brace. All that mattered was this girl, this beautiful, heavenly creature standing before him, smiling. Smiles were rare those days, more rare than anyone knew, at least for him.

"Hi there, soldier," she fairly whispered, and his cheeks seared as though branded. "What's your name?"

"Bill. Bill McInnes" he stammered, his voice sounding foreign in his ears, a buzzing sound ringing there instead.

"My name's Claire. Claire Steinmetz. Glad to make your acquaintance." Her hand reached out, and he took it, the soft, velvety skin warm against his palm. "Maybe I'll see you around here again?"

"Maybe." That sounded stupid. Why couldn't he say something original, witty, like Johnny? But she smiled anyway. She'd said she hoped she'd see him around. He'd make sure she did. This girl, her softness and warmth, was what he needed, what he wanted more than anything else in all the mixed up, broken-down world. Just watching her glide down the wooden walkway gave him hope, and then it happened: She turned, looked over her right shoulder, and wiggled a coy little wave toward him with her fingers. The wave didn't matter, but the look did. She had turned to look back.

Hope flew away as she turned the corner. It was promptly replaced with prayer, prayer that he would indeed see her again. Seeing her again was all that mattered. It would be his salvation, he was sure. After everything, all the disappointments, all the pain, something wonderful and magical had happened, even if only for a few moments. He had to see her again, no matter what.

chapter 2

By the time dinner rolled around on Thursday evening, I was bleary-eyed and exhausted. It had been a wildly busy, irritating day and, because I'd read the book in one sitting the night before, I'd had very little sleep. We'd had a press go down, and the evening edition had been just a little late, about thirty minutes, but enough to cause every phone in the building to ring with questions from subscribers about where their paper was and when it would be delivered. I can't understand why the switchboard would route calls up to the features desk, but they did. I'd been expecting a call from a college dean with whom I'd requested an interview for a story, and I was just positive he'd called and couldn't get through, so my aggravation meter was pegged. When the clock hit four-thirty, I damn near broke the glass busting through the double doors to get out of the building. The restaurant was only a couple of blocks away, and I tried to keep from breaking into a run, afraid someone would call my name. I couldn't handle one more detail.

I asked the maitre d' about the guys, and he pointed me to the back. Michael was already there, his wavy, blond mane barely grazing the top of those broad shoulders, ready for the season. I knew those tanned arms would be glad to get out of the fluorescent lighting of the Y and back onto the whitewater down on the river. Must be nice to have a job where your biggest wardrobe question is, *How close to naked can I be today without scraping off half my skin?* I was guessing he had been spending a lot of his time lately interviewing and trying out guides for the rafting expedition company. He especially liked trying out the female guides. I'm not sure any of them actually knew what they were doing, but if they had enough top-end buoyancy to keep Michael above them for a couple of hours once or twice a week, they had a job for sure. I wouldn't have put it past him to check out the guys too. Michael just took it as it came and rarely, if ever, turned it down, regardless what it was. Grab a dictionary and look up "free spirit." His picture is probably there.

Jim was there too, sucking on a straw. Even though he idolized Michael, who'd already had a mai-tai, he'd stuck to a soft drink. He seemed nervous, but then Jim always seemed nervous. A drink might have done him good. He looked forward to the trips every year, though he was a teeth-gnashing, hand-wringing wreck by the time we left. It was hard for him to keep up with us sometimes, his short, chubby legs pumping and his round, bald head breaking out into a four-quart sweat, but he really tried. He got overly excited and almost hyperventilated if Russ promised he'd get laid on a trip. I felt sorry for him because it was such a long time between trips, and I was pretty sure that was the only time he ever got any, but he seemed okay with it. When he was shaken he started stuttering, so someone would have to kind of translate for him, but he didn't seem to mind that either. I guess if I wore a suit all day every day and spent all my time consoling the relatives of the dearly departed, I'd get excited at the prospect of a live body too, and I sure wouldn't mind someone explaining to a nice-looking, twenty-three-year-old topless dancer that I was on vacation and needed some companionship. His line of work was bound to be hard, but everyone needs a mortician sooner or later, and business was booming. He'd just purchased another piece of land and, when the new one was completed, he would be the owner of five funeral parlors, none in town but rather in the little hamlets around us, places no one else thought worth their time. More than once I'd heard him say, "Quality over quantity," but he was experiencing both, and times were good. One time while he was embalming an old guy, he'd found a quarter in the fellow's underwear. "See, there's money in dead bodies," he'd nervously giggled. He wasn't kidding. The new Jaguar he'd ordered proved it. But he sure wasn't anybody's idea of a babe magnet, car or no car.

"Hey, Steve, over here!" he shouted in a loud, artificially cheerful greeting across the room. A couple of people turned to look. I just smiled. Sometimes it's nice to know you're popular with someone, even if it is just Jim.

"Anybody seen Russ?" I asked instantly, pulling up my chair. The waiter popped the cap off a cold one and set it on the table in front of me. The first drag was chilled and foamy. I felt life creeping back into my veins and the tension in my neck began to fade.

"No," Michael sighed. "I hope he shows up pretty soon. I left work early for this. Two excellent prospects, a redhead and a brunette, and I left them for Alex to interview. This had better be good." He took another sip of his cocktail, at the same time flicking his cigarette ashes into the ashtray.

"What's he got in mind this year? A safari? An off-shore fishing trip? Maybe looking for a sunken galleon?" Jim gushed, clasping and unclasping his hands quickly, his fingers flailing about in the air. You'd think it were a scout trip or something, the way his face was smeared with glee.

"I have no idea," I answered in a pensive tone, not sure if I should repeat our conversation. "But I think it has something to do with . . ."

"Guys!" Russ was all grins, pulling up his chair and plopping down in it, his eyes darting back and forth. "Hey, Steve," he grinned, "you've put on a couple of pounds since last year. And it's been snowing right above your ears too, buddy!"

"Thanks, Russ," I spat toward him. "You don't look a day younger this year either. You've never taken us to the fountain of youth on one of these trips. When might we expect that?"

"Yeah, I'm all for that," Michael chimed in. "It's getting harder and harder for me to attract quality employees," he frowned. "Guess they think the 'fringe benefits' aren't as good as they would be with some of my younger coworkers. So, for crying out loud, don't rag Steve about his age."

I thought I was going to have to clock both of them. "What's the deal with my age? I'm just a couple of years older than either of you. And I look a few younger." Well, it was true. I did. My hair was longer and darker than ever and, despite the graying at the temples, I still had all of it, unlike Russ. I worked out four times a week. My only negative dietary vice was beer, and I managed to consume a fairly healthy diet otherwise. Mom's Hispanic heritage gave me smooth, dark skin, with hardly a wrinkle. Because of the history of heart disease and cancer in my dad's family, I had a great number of possible health issues with which to be concerned, but my age had never been an issue. We Rileys tended to live long, healthy lives, and I was in better shape, looked better, than when I was thirty. Jealous assholes.

"Okay, okay," Russ retreated, stroking his hand both slowly and vainly across his shiny head. "So I'm a client of 'Hair Club,'" he chuckled. "Let's get down to business. I've got a great idea for this year's trip."

"Fantastic!" Jim fairly stuttered, his cheeks rosy with excitement. "What is it, where are we going?"

"Well, that's part of the problem," he smirked. "I'm not really sure just yet. I've got some of my people working on it." His people, right. He's an artist in a graphics shop, for god's sake. What people? "I know a guy who knows a guy, and he's . . ."

"Oh, cut the crap, Russ," Michael interrupted, the effects of the drink kicking in. "What the hell is it? Where are we going?" He seemed a bit irritated, like a kid opening a gift on which Mom had used way too much really sticky tape.

"That's just it," he replied. "Did you read the book, Steve? Like I asked you to? Did you guys read it too? What did you think of it?"

By now I was getting a little testy myself. "Yes, Russ. I read the book."

"And what did you think of it?" he repeated, looking out at me from under his brows with a goofy smile pulling up one corner of his mouth. Confusion clouded Michael and Jim's faces.

"Well, honestly," I hesitated, "I liked it. I didn't think I would, but I did. I was, well, maybe, enthralled? I just couldn't put it down. I don't know how to describe it," I admitted, stumbling and stammering for words to explain, to express how I'd felt. It was a little embarrassing, sounding like a thirty-six-year-old housewife describing one of those paperback romance novels.

"What about you guys? Jim, what did you think?" he asked innocently.

"I loved it," Jim gushed, wringing his hands. "I'd love that Claire, just like that Bill guy did. But I'd never leave her," he added, looking as if he were about to cry, remembering the story.

"What about you, Michael?" Russ turned his attention to Michael, who was becoming visibly frustrated.

"What the hell difference does it make, Russ?" he exploded. "Let's talk about the damn trip, okay? That's what we came here for, isn't it?"

Russ laughed out loud, teasing the three of us with his eyes. "How would you like to be the first people to meet Nick Roberts, the author of the book?"

"Nobody knows who he is," Jim offered loudly. "Nobody. No one's ever met him. They don't know anything about him."

"What if I told you that we could find him?" Russ asked softly, leaning over the table like an international spy planning an act of espionage.

"Oh, hell, Russ, what have you got up your sleeve?" I blurted out, tired of the cloak-and-dagger bullshit. "What's this all about?"

"Well, it seems my brother's best friend is working for the publishing house that produced *The Celtic Fan*," he answered quietly. He cast a few anxious glances around to see if anyone at one of the other tables were listening. "He can find out where Nick Roberts lives. Then we could go out and find him. Think about it, Steve. What a great feature for your paper. A great piece, don't you think? And you guys," he said, pointing at Michael and Jim, "could say you'd met him, get his autograph and stuff. Have your picture made with him. Wouldn't that be something?"

Tempting. Very tempting. There had to be a catch.

"So, what's the catch?" I quizzed, afraid I was about to be sold a chunk of the Berlin wall again. Probably had something to do with paying the brother off somehow or, worse yet, taking him along.

"No catch," he insisted, trying to maintain a look of dignity and honesty. That was hard work for Russ. "My brother's working on finding the information on the location, and the rest is up to us. Are you guys in?"

"Well, I guess so," Jim responded, halting between words. "Maybe he can introduce us to the woman he modeled Claire's character after." Good old Jim, thinking about his annual conquest. Or at least his annual attempt.

"What about you, Michael?" he asked as he turned and stared into Michael's tipsy face. "Are you in?"

"Sure, sure," Michael sputtered, his speech somewhat slurred by the liquor. "Sounds good to me."

"Steve? You with us?" It was hard for me to answer, my tongue sticking to the roof of my mouth, my head buzzing. Meet Nick Roberts, the guy who'd written with such passion and imagination, the one who'd described the relationship between Bill and Claire with such power, such intensity, that I found myself longing to be with them, to be part of the love and energy they'd experienced. A writer whose work had affected me like no one else's before, at least not in a long, long time.

"Um, you bet. You bet," was all I could manage. I couldn't wait to pack my suitcase, hop in a cab, and roll right up to his front door. This would be great. "Count me in," I almost whispered.

"Okay! Good! I'll tell Dave to proceed, and maybe we'll have enough information by the end of next week to move forward with our plans." He seemed pleased with himself. Unlike most times, he also looked sure, as though he knew this would be a doable thing. "I'll let you know as soon as I get something concrete."

"I propose a toast," Jim nearly shouted. In total synchronization, the three of us threw our fingers up to our lips, shushing him. "I propose a toast," he began again, quieter, lifting his soft drink glass above the center of the table. "To Nick Roberts. May we be as surprised as he will be when we find him."

Well, I hope to shout, I thought to myself as our glasses and bottles clinked together. I took a deep drag on the longneck. If we could pull this off, we'd be famous. And I'd have a great feature.

We were going to find Nick Roberts. We would succeed. We would meet him, and I would understand his talent. Maybe some of it would rub off on me. No matter what happened, I'd never be the same, of that I was sure.

I couldn't possibly have known how correct that assumption would prove to be.

The dance was almost over and still he sat, worshiping her radiance from across the room. It had seemed ridiculous to come in the first place, to subject himself to that kind of torture. She kept looking over at him, as though she expected him to stand and walk,

straight and tall, across the room and ask her to dance. The last dance was announced, and the thing he feared most began to unfold. She strode across the room confidently and, bending to look directly into his face, asked the question he dreaded: "Well, Bill, will you dance with me or not? I've waited all night."

He wanted to scream, to run, but he couldn't move, couldn't get the damn leg to work that fast. Before he could protest, she grabbed his hands and pulled him to his feet. Panic flooded over him, and he grabbed for the crutches. But something magical saved the moment, something eternal and precious.

Claire's right arm wrapped around his neck, and she took his right hand in her left. "You don't need those," she announced, her voice firm and resolute. "I'll steady you, I promise. Just relax and enjoy, could you please?" Her cheeks were pink, her smile warm, and his apprehension began to fade. She leaned into him, but not so far as to throw him off balance, and they swayed gently to the beat. The music ended, and still they swayed, isolated from the rest of the revelers, unaware that most everyone was gone, that they danced to a tune only they could hear.

"We need to turn out the lights now," a man's voice called from the outskirts of the tent, and they stopped, gazing into each other's eyes, a steady understanding growing between them. Moving toward the chairs, she picked up his crutches. As he took them, she leaned forward and whispered into his ear, "I don't see a soldier in a brace, struggling along on crutches. I see a very brave, very handsome man who's made a great sacrifice. For that, I'm truly blessed." Then suddenly, she placed a gentle kiss on his cheek and, just as quickly, she was gone. But not that kiss, pressed permanently into his skin. He could feel it the next morning, still there, soft and sweet. It just wouldn't go away.

chapter 3

R uss called on Sunday afternoon. I could almost feel his excitement through the phone.

"My brother's friend at New Century Publishing got into the acquisitions manager's office," he began in breathless explanation. "He got the guy's password and got into his files. Know what he found?"

"Isn't that illegal, Russ?" I pondered aloud, ignoring his question, trying hard to throw him. He pressed on.

"Oh, illegal, hell. Anyway, he checked disbursements for advances. He found an account number for Nick Roberts. He went back down to his own desk and hacked into the accounting files. They've been mailing Roberts' checks to a post office box in North Carolina, some little hole in the wall near Cherokee or Asheville or one of those southwestern cities," he explained.

"So you've got the address, right?" I quizzed, beginning to share his excitement.

"Well, not exactly," he answered. "I've got to find someone at the post office who will tell me the address of the person the box belongs to. But I'm sure that's not going to be a problem."

I was pretty sure he was right. After all, we were talking about postal workers. And I was getting really wired. "So what now?" I asked, ready to do whatever was needed.

"I'll get back to you in a couple of days, or as soon as I get the information," Russ promised. "In the meantime, get ready to go to North Carolina."

"No problem," I almost screamed. Russ was serious now, and I was confident we'd get the information we needed. It was just a matter of time. "Call me. Don't forget, call me as soon as you know," I repeated.

"You call Michael and I'll call Jim," he said. "Talk to you soon."

Soon was sooner than I imagined. My phone rang on Monday afternoon, and the "What?" I answered with was meant for Jerry in the composing room who called every day at about that time. I was surprised to hear Russ's voice on the other end.

"Got it," he said. "We have a street address. Well, it's most likely a gravel road, but it's an actual address."

"So? Details," I demanded.

"So it shows up as belonging to a woman," Russ reported. "Could be a girlfriend, I suppose. Maybe his mom. Or maybe she's his wife, kept her family name. I don't know. But whoever she is, she's getting his money, so we can at least look into it, right?"

"Absolutely," I agreed, thinking about how we should go about it. "What's the plan from this point?"

"Um, I'm not sure," Russ admitted. "I'm hoping you can help me with this part of it. I think the big thing to remember is that no one can know what we're up to. We don't want someone else jumping in."

"True," I agreed. "Since we think this place is pretty rural, could we fake a camping trip, or maybe hiking, or something like that?"

"You're brilliant! Especially for an old guy," Russ laughed. Not very funny. "Let's meet again and finalize the plans. Tomorrow night? Same time and place as before?"

"Sure. I'll call Michael," I offered, "and you call Jim."

"Done. See you then," he chirped as he dropped the receiver.

There was a ton of hiking and camping gear in my garage, and it wouldn't take a lot of work to get it cleaned up, or should it be clean? After all, wouldn't our hiking trip look more authentic if our equipment was dusty and messed up? Shouldn't we go into town separately? Or should someone go first and scope things out? That seemed like the best way to get to the locals. Maybe we could even get directions from someone who lived nearby. There were so many things to consider, but the important element was surprise. No one could know what we were up to, no one. We had to be very, very careful.

It was amazing how big this Roberts issue really was. I'd mentioned the book earlier in the week in the office break room and every head turned. Hell, conversations across the room came to a screeching halt and all the buzz turned toward me. I found myself wishing my pieces generated that much talk. One guy said he'd seen a posting on a website offering a reward to the first person who located Nick Roberts. Not much cash, he'd reported, but it would probably pay expenses, maybe a few thousand dollars. A woman from the photography department said she'd heard there were at least two hundred people actively searching for Roberts, but so far no luck. They all said reports were that he'd managed to cover his tracks about as well as Howard Hughes. I just couldn't have guessed how many people had gotten caught up in the mystery surrounding the elusive Nick Roberts. There were at least twenty-five people in the break room, and every one of them seemed to know all about the book. And they were all so different, everyone from the geeky mail room guy to a suit from accounting to that really slick, stacked, cheerleader-turned-contributing editor from the news desk. They'd all read it, and they all wanted to know more about this mystery man.

I did too. The more I knew, the more I wanted to know. The more difficult it seemed to track this guy down, the more I wanted to find him. And the more I wanted to find him, the more I wondered about something.

If I found him, would I want to tell?

Sitting outside the big house in the old Buick, Bill stared at the windows, hoping to catch a glimpse of her before he went to the door. Her parents most certainly wouldn't eat him, but he really didn't want to take any chances. His first impression had to be a good one. No room to mess up this time.

The doorbell could be heard for a country mile, he was sure. Expecting her father to open the door, he slicked back his hair again. But when the door flew open, Claire stood there, somewhat flushed and hurried.

"Come on, let's go. Hurry!" She flew down the steps, rushing him along. What's this all about?, *he wondered.*

"Claire, what's wrong? Did I do something wrong?" he asked, fearing he'd broken some unspoken rule, made himself unwelcome without knowledge of his indiscretion.

"No, it's not you," she replied, blushing. "I'll explain later. Let's just try to enjoy ourselves, okay?"

"That'll be easy," Bill smiled, cranking the old engine to life and pulling away from the house. He thought he saw a face in the front window, stern and disapproving. She would reveal all later, he was sure. But the face chewed at his brain, constantly on the fringe of the evening, threatening the joy he felt just being in her presence.

chapter 4

When we met again the next night. I'd already made up my mind to one thing. Regardless what happened, I wanted us to split up when we got to our destination. I had plenty to think about and decisions to make. Most importantly, I wanted to be completely and totally prepared when I met Nick Roberts, wanted to know exactly what I was going to say and how.

Jim was just about goofy with anxiety by the time we got there. Before I could even greet him, he gushed, "Maybe the woman is Claire! You think? You think? Maybe?"

"Hi to you too, Jim," I replied flatly, settling into my chair, note pad in hand. "Michael here yet?"

"Yep," he answered, turning to look at the bar. "Up there, at the far end. See?"

Sure, I saw. He was leaning on the bar, trying his dead-level best to look charming, staring back into the face of a brunette. Looking at her from behind made me want to go and stare into her face too. If that was the first view he'd had of her, no wonder he was knocking himself out. He glanced at me, made his "just one second" gesture, and handed the great backside something, probably his phone number. As he made his way over to the table, I noticed that she never turned around to see where he was going. Poor Michael – obviously losing his touch. I made up my mind right then and there that if I ever cut off my hair, I'd give the ponytail to him. Couldn't hurt his chances any.

"So, did Whitewater Dude score?" I chuckled, remembering some of the things he'd said about me in the past.

"Hey, I took up for you last time, pal, so don't rib me," he answered, looking at his beer instead of me. "Forty-six hasn't been too good to me. I didn't see you even trying."

"Ah, I gave it up after Donna," I reminded him. It was true. I hadn't dated in over a year. I didn't know how many opportunities had passed me by, and I didn't even care anymore. She'd burned me and burned me good, and I was still toasty around the edges. Those games, I'd concluded, were for the younger guys. Four weeks of antibiotics and a big blow-out when I confronted her were enough, but the real kicker was the guy she was cheating with, one of my old college buddies she'd met at my reunion. Bitch. I needed that like I needed another communicable disease. My next relationship needed to be recently released from a convent for having been celibate too long. My kinda woman.

"Here comes Russ," Jim stammered, so excited he was breathless. "He looks really happy. I hope he's got good news."

Russ had an armload of stuff, pieces of paper sticking out all over the place. "I've got all the information we need right here," he announced without even offering a greeting. "Ready to hear it?"

"No, we came here to sit around for a couple of hours and play group solitaire," Michael snorted, lighting another cigarette as soon as he dropped the first butt in his empty glass.

"Wise guy, huh?" Russ retorted. "Here goes. It's 19 Creekside Road in Ebbs Mill. I got the address from a postal worker, sure enough. It wasn't hard at all. I just had to promise him fifty dollars when I get there. Trusting soul. I don't even remember what I told him to get him to talk."

If he knew Russ, he wouldn't have made that deal.

"So I called a local realtor," he continued, "and told her I was moving, asked to see some property for sale in the area. She said she'd show me around when I get into town. That means I have an excuse to check out the area."

"Where does that leave us?" I asked.

"Well, you guys can chill out somewhere in town until I get some idea where we're supposed to be. Steve, what did you come up with as far as finding the place?"

"I've got plenty of camping and hiking equipment," I offered. "There's more than enough to go around between the four of us. I'm thinking maybe we'll get a map of the area. And then, once we've seen the area, we'll use the map, split up the area, and each of us can search a portion. Maybe one of us will see something or someone and make contact with the resident. A woman, you said?"

"That's the information I've got," Russ confirmed. "Shouldn't we use a motel or something as a base?"

"I'll use the motel as a base," Jim giggled, lifting his beer again. Why we kept bringing him along was beyond me. Pity, maybe. "I wonder if the woman is Claire?" he added again, grinning.

"Her name is Diana Frazier. Doesn't exactly sound like Claire to me," Russ responded, almost allowing disgust to creep into his tone. "I've got the name of a motel, the Blue Bell Inn, and it's really the only one close by. I can make the arrangements, get adjoining rooms if they've got them. Sound okay?"

"Sounds okay to me," Michael said, disinterest obvious in his voice. "You sure we're going to find this Roberts fellow?"

"Yeah, I'm pretty sure. You in, Steve?" he asked with a broad grin.

"Sure." I was feeling generous. "Jim can room with me. That okay with you, Jim?"

"Oh, absolutely. I can hardly wait. Is this a very big place, lots of people to meet?" he asked, twiddling his thumbs frantically and painting a stiff smirk on his face. As if we couldn't figure out what he was thinking.

"No, 'fraid not," Russ admitted, not even acknowledging Jim's motives. "This is a small town. We've got to be very, very cautious. Four guys descending on a small town will make people wonder what we're up to unless we cover our tracks." He took out a map. "See this? This is the national forest, Great Smoky Mountains National Park, and here's the town," he explained, pointing first to the green, unevenly-shaped figure on the map and then to a small dot. "Here's the story: I've invited the three of you to hike with me while I'm on a trip to find a place to live because I'm being transferred, you know, a job thing."

"What kind of job? Where?" Michael taunted.

"Does it matter?" Russ snapped back. "I'll figure out something to tell the realtor. Maybe I can find a local industry, tell her I'm considering a job offer there. I don't know."

"What, the local corn pone or red flannel shirt factory? What if there are only seventy-five employees and she's related to sixty-nine of them?" Michael snickered, finding himself amusing.

Russ ignored him. "You'll help me figure this out, right, Steve?"

"Absolutely," I assured him. For the first time in a long time, I was getting more than just a little excited. This actually seemed possible, and I could begin to imagine it happening, having my picture made with Roberts. Even better, I could imagine sitting with him on a stump in a clearing, a faded, rickety, white clapboard cottage in the background, talking about the book, the characters, and his writing style. I could see him pulling out a copy of the book and autographing it. I'm not impressed with autographs, but I'd take it, and I'd promise I'd never tell a soul who he was or where he was. Even the story I'd tell the guys was beginning to gel: I didn't find him. No luck at all, just some guy living in a little house in a little podunk town. We've been looking in the wrong place. Let's just forget this and go home. Me, maintaining his anonymity. Me, maintaining a rapport with him, and eventually he steps out of obscurity and into the limelight with his second or third book, and I'm his good, good friend. Everyone finds out that I know him, and they all envy me. Then maybe I could sell a book deal or two, get him to write the foreword. Book publishers, agents, I'm in all over the place. This could be really big.

"Steve? Steve, you with us?" Russ and Michael were staring at me. I'd just drifted away, a long way away. Jim had begun to look a little pale, the apprehension taking over.

"Of course. Just thinking," I stammered, a little embarrassed. "Let's do it. I'm ready. When are we leaving?"

"I can be ready by Monday. Michael?"

"I'm good to go by then. You guys okay with that?"

"I can be," I promised. "Jim, is that okay with you?"

"Uh, we're really going?"

"Yes," I answered firmly. "We're really going. Are you going with us?"

"Um-hum," he almost whispered, growing more pale and sweaty by the minute. "Sure. I'm going. I can be ready by Monday." I slapped him on the back. That seemed to bring some blood back to his face. In fact, he blushed, apparently aware of his outward signs of trepidation.

"Okay then," Russ announced. "It'll take about two and a half hours to get there from here. We'll leave Monday morning, eight o'clock."

It was done. We were going. And I promised myself that I would be the one to meet Nick Roberts. There was zero doubt in my mind that the victor would be me.

"What do you mean, McInnes?" He paced the floor, brow furrowed and face fire red. "You know how we feel about this, Claire. How could you? I forbid you to see him. Forbid it!"

"But Daddy!" she began, tears trickling down her perfect cheeks, leaving trails in the dust of her powder. "Please, you don't underst . . ."

"Don't understand? Who do you think you are? You have no idea what happened when my grandmother married my grandfather. It was a nightmare, a disaster. The families were broken apart for years. It took decades for things to get back to some semblance of normalcy. And you tell me I don't understand?" He shook his head, sat down beside her, and took her hands in his. "Claire, if you marry outside the Jewish faith, you know what kind of turmoil will be caused in the family. There are dozens of young men around here, nice Jewish boys, not some Scotch-Irish crippled-up trash you found . . ."

"I won't listen to any more of this!" Leaping up from the sofa, she ran up the stairs, slamming the door behind her, knocking the pictures on the hallway wall askew and rattling the china in the

dining room cabinet. He hated to do this, to try to forbid a girl her age to see someone, but it was necessary. It would save them all immeasurable heartache in the long run.

Across her bed, handkerchief soaked, Claire formulated a way to see the dashing soldier, the fine, brave man with whom she realized she was beginning to fall in love.

chapter 5

Monday morning's sun was bright and hot. It was the second week of April and already it was warming up like the middle of summer. I had everything ready, and Russ brought over the SUV he'd rented for the occasion. There was plenty of room in the back. We stuffed my suitcase in the rear by the bag Russ brought, as well as all the equipment we'd be using for our cover.

We stopped at Michael's to pick him up. He didn't seem too happy. The bag he'd packed was huge, and I imagined it full of cigarettes and whiskey.

"What the hell have you got in there, Michael? Your second cousin?" Russ sniped, chuckling under his breath.

"You know, I didn't want to say anything in front of Jim. You know how he gets," Michael started, "but I have serious doubts that this idiot scheme is going to work." A look of condescending sarcasm covered his face, and I could tell Russ was bristling. "What's the big deal about this Roberts guy anyway?"

"Hey, Michael, you loaned me the damn book, remember?" It took great restraint to keep my voice even, my tone non-confrontational, and still get the point across. "We've been talking about this for a good while now. If you didn't want to go, why didn't you say so? It's going to work. Do you still want to go? You can back out right now." I could feel Russ getting ready to blow, and I knew I'd be right behind him if we didn't get this out in the open. Worst-case scenario would've been Michael starting this conversation half-way there in the SUV, which was his typical way of dealing with things. Then if it all fell apart, it wasn't his fault, because he'd let us know at some point that he didn't really want to go. "Gonna bail? Well, speak up."

It was the first time somebody had pinned him down. "No. I'll go. I'm in," he answered haltingly, looking at everything but us.

"Okay then," I replied, forcing an authoritative tone into my voice. "Let's go. Jim's expecting us." I could feel Russ relaxing, calming somewhat. He slipped into the driver's seat. I took the front passenger seat, and Michael took the back driver's side position.

Jim was waiting on the sidewalk, bag in hand. He stressed over the way we put his suitcase in the back. It wasn't as large as Michael's, but it was extremely heavy. "Got books in here?" I asked him, remembering how heavy even a small box of books seemed when I moved the last time. The sound of pills rattling in tiny plastic bottles escaped through the canvas.

"Uh, yeah, books," he answered hesitantly. Then it hit me: Magazines. He was taking his stash with him, probably to look at in the bathroom. I almost laughed out loud imagining that the pills I heard were for erectile dysfunction. I had this feeling he wouldn't hike the area like we'd agreed to do.

"All set?" Russ asked over his right shoulder. No one said otherwise, and he pulled away from the curb, headed toward I-40 and the mountains already visible in the distance. In just a few minutes, we were outside the Knoxville city limits and on our way.

The drive was uneventful, unless you count the times we stopped for Jim to get out and "breathe," whatever that means. The mountains were beautiful, clouds still hanging halfway down their waking slopes, trees budding everywhere in shades of yellow, green, and pink. The sun hid behind a cloud, then crept back out, then hid again, a peek-a-boo game all the way. We arrived in Ebbs Mill right at lunchtime. The sign at the edge of town read "Population 210," and from the looks of things that might've been a little optimistic of them. I was a bit concerned, considering most of the weddings I've attended drew crowds larger than the number of residents in this wide spot in the road. No wonder there was only one motel in town which, of course, was easy to locate. There was a big cast iron bell out front hanging from a huge frame and it was painted bright blue, making it the obvious namesake of the motel. Russ checked in at the office and picked up two keys for our "suite," which we would soon discover was really a tiny little house attached to the end of the motel. It even had a tiny little kitchen. Unfortunately, it did not have two bathrooms, nor did it have precious works of art on the walls or a push-button phone, which was a shame because cell reception was almost non-existent there. In fact, clean and dry was all I could say for it, but we weren't there for the lodging amenities anyway. We were there to find Nick Roberts. I kept reminding myself of that as Jim and Michael fought over who would get which room.

Russ found a spot in the room where he at least had a couple of bars and called the realtor. She was out of the office, and her secretary promised she would return his call. The next order of business was to find something to eat. We'd spotted a streaky-windowed diner on the way in and decided to try it. It was that or the convenience store at the other end of town, where the motel owner had assured Russ we could find a submarine sandwich and cold drinks. That would work when we'd tired of the diner's fare. We piled in the car, all except Michael. "Think I'll stay here," he announced. "I'm not too hungry." He was probably just thirsty. I would've paid five bucks to find out what was in that suitcase.

We slid into a booth and started to look at the menu, and Jim was already stressing. "Do they have something low cholesterol? Maybe I should have a salad," he whispered. He looked a little sallow. I was busy looking at the offerings, which were classic diner picks. The special was meatloaf, complete with gravy-soaked mashed potatoes and green beans. There were burgers, including slawburgers, which kind of made me queasy at the thought. The best choice looked like the fried chicken. Russ seemed to be having a hard time choosing. "Just exactly what is 'chicken-fried steak?'" he queried.

"I think it's the left-over stuff that won't fit into nuggets," I snickered. He didn't look amused, but rather slightly alarmed. "It was just a joke, Russ," I assured him. "I think it's probably perfectly safe. They have liver and onions too."

"Oh, for the love of . . . Maybe I'll just have a burger," he replied, disdain written across his face. I had to admit, the convenience store didn't look too bad at that moment.

"I just want a salad, that's all. Just a salad, no dressing," Jim fidgeted, turning the menu over and over. I stifled the urge to reach across and grab it, snatch it out of his hands, maybe even hold them still so they wouldn't wiggle so much.

The waitress walked up, a round, reddish woman of about fifty with big hair and lots of makeup, and said abruptly, "Know what you want?" She was already tapping the pencil on her order pad before one of us could answer.

"I'll have the fried chicken plate," I answered without hesitation. "And a glass of tea, unsweetened."

"Nope. Sweet is the only way it comes," she answered curtly. "What'll you have, sir?" she spoke toward Jim without looking up.

"Just a salad, no dressing. Just a plain salad," he restated.

She looked at him with a stiff smirk. "Plain? Just lettuce? Or would you like some other stuff in it, like tomatoes, or carrots, or radishes? Maybe cucumbers? Because that's how we make it. I'm not sure the chef will pick out the other stuff for you. You might have to do that yourself if you don't want it." She used this annoying, lilting, nasal tone to get her point across, and she emphasized the term chef, trying to be smug and snide. It worked. Jim was as flustered as I'd seen him in a long time.

"Um, just, um, it doesn't matter, uh, just a salad, however you, um, however you make it," he stuttered. I was beginning to get just a little warm under the collar watching her make sport of him. "And a glass of tea just like his," he motioned toward me. She looked at me. I didn't smile.

She turned to Russ. "And what for you, sir?"

"Well, I could order roast strips of diner slut, but I'm afraid it would be kind of tough," he grinned mockingly. She grew a little redder. That coaxed a shudder from me, thinking of all the stories I'd been told about things restaurant employees do to the food of disagreeable patrons before they serve it. "But I think I'll have the fried chicken plate too. No variations, no difficulties. Just like it's printed here. And tea too, just like theirs."

She turned and walked away, stomping a bit as she went. Jim still looked a little upset, staring at his fork, pushing the tines down so the handle popped up and down, up and down. Russ was quiet.

"Damn, I hope if she decides to spit in someone's food that she picks yours," I said, a little hint of worry creeping out.

"We've got bigger fish to fry, my friends," Russ smiled. "Let's talk about what we're going to do this afternoon. I'm going with the realtor. I'm wondering . . . Steve, want to go with me? That way more than one of us would know where things are around here."

"Sure, I'll go." I'd jump at the chance. Copious amounts of time spent with Michael and Jim in the motel didn't look too entertaining. About that time an elderly gent, tall and thin, kind of stooped, stopped at the end of the table. His hands were big and calloused, and his plaid flannel shirt was faded and worn under the pale blue, stress-frayed overalls that hung on his gaunt frame.

"You guys visitin' 'round here?" he asked in typical nosy small town fashion.

"Yep," Russ answered. "I'm looking to move here. Getting transferred with my job."

"Really?" the old fellow asked, looking confused. "Just where do you work?"

"Well, actually, the job is in Asheville," Russ continued to bluff. "But property is so high there, I thought maybe I'd just commute. Any really nice places for sale around here?"

"Not that I know of," the fellow replied.

"Anything new being built? Any elite areas cropping up, because I don't want to sound snobbish, but I make pretty good money. Any famous people living around here?" Russ threw in. I knew he was fishing now.

"Nope," the old guy said, shaking his head. "Nobody of any consequence livin' 'round here. Just a buncha farmers and ole folks. A few young 'uns, but just a few. Nothin' new bein' built. We got a real estate lady, though. Maybe you should ask her," he offered.

"I've got an appointment with her later," Russ volunteered, "but I thought I'd just ask a local, you know, someone with nothing to gain. Sometimes you get the best information that way, about property and such."

"Sorry I can't be of more help," the man shrugged. "But I hope y'all enjoy your visit. This is a pretty place. And the people are friendly too." He smiled and walked away. I was a little surprised that he was a local and yet obviously hadn't met our waitress.

"Hear that?" Russ whispered. "No one famous living here, nothing new being built. No expensive areas. He's hiding out real good."

"Or he's not here," Jim frowned, still playing with the flatware. I had to admit I thought a local would know about Nick Roberts. Or maybe he did, and just wasn't talking. Maybe they had all taken a vow to help him maintain his anonymity if he'd stay there and pump some money into the local tax base.

When our food came, it wasn't too bad. The fried chicken was actually edible and somewhat enjoyable. None of us said much. We were busy thinking. When we finished, I left a generous tip by my plate. All my life I'd heard that old saying, "You can catch more flies with honey than you can with vinegar," and I thought it was possible we might need some help from Helga the

Kitchen Wench before this was all over. We paid at the cash register, but not before she had run to our table and begun to clear it off. She called behind us, "You guys come back!" in a much more cheerful tone than she'd used taking our orders. The tip had paid off.

Back at the Blue Bell Motel, Michael had passed out and was snoring noisily across the bed, but not before he had taken a message from the realtor on the cell Russ had accidentally left behind. Russ called her back. I tried not to listen to the conversation, but I could tell he was heaping on the charm. When he hung up the phone, he found me in the room I was sharing with Jim, hanging up my clothes and making the best of the arrangements.

"She said she'd come by in about thirty minutes and pick us up," he reported. "She said it would just work out better if she drove, because she knows where she's going." That made sense to me. I wondered what Russ had said to her, and hoped that the story he told her matched the one he'd used in the diner with the old man.

Twenty-five minutes later, she knocked on the door. Russ was visibly taken aback. She was about thirty-five and shapely in a soft, round, over-the-top feminine kind of way, with dark hair and dark eyes. My best guess was that she was part Cherokee, the Native Americans who lived in the North Carolina town of the same name nearby. Russ introduced us, and I shook her hand. Firm grip.

"Leonard Russell, but everyone calls me Russ. Nice to meet you," he stammered, openly looking her over. "And this is my friend, Steve Riley."

"I'm Cherilyn McDonald. Nice to meet you," she gushed, and she looked directly into my eyes when she spoke to me. Out of the corner of my eye I could see Russ looking slightly put out. Was it my fault he looked like an aging Opie Taylor?

"Nice to meet you too," I said, trying to remain as disinterested as possible. "Shouldn't we be going?"

"Oh, sure," she winked, and led the way out the door. Russ growled under his breath, "I'm sitting in the front, so don't even think about it!"

"No problem," I grinned, whispering back. "I'm not interested. Go for it."

He practically skipped to the car and jumped in. She asked where we wanted to go first, and Russ flashed a winsome smile. "Oh, just surprise us," he said. We drove around for nearly twenty minutes, being treated to a guided tour of the tiny hamlet. She pointed out the mayor's house, the two churches, Baptist and Methodist, and the elementary school. "Kids, Russ?" she asked.

"No, afraid not," he replied. "I'm divorced."

"Isn't your wife a little worried about you running around with this bachelor, Steve?" she grinned, looking back at me in the rearview mirror.

"I'm not married," I answered hesitantly. Russ shot me a threatening look. I shrugged. What was I supposed to do, create a wife?

"Really?" she shrilled, apparently delighted. Great. The realtor had the hots for me, and Russ was mad about it.

"Never have been. I'm not that crazy about women," I lied. Russ stretched, put his arms up and his hands behind his head, and gave me a double thumbs up out of her field of vision. Peace reigned.

"Oh, that's too bad," she sighed. "I have a sister I'd love to introduce you to if you change your mind." That meant I'd effectively screwed myself out of meeting another attractive woman, one Russ didn't already have his eye on. Swell, just swell. My best bet was to act invisible and stare out the car window.

"So what do you do for a living, Russ?" Cherilyn inquired.

Oh, no. An opportunity for Russ to talk about himself. "Well, I'm in corporate marketing," he explained. I almost laughed. He draws cartoons for advertisements. Since when is that corporate marketing? Great imagination. Cherilyn cooed, oohed, and aahhed. Russ rattled on.

"I wouldn't mind having a small house, maybe something older. It doesn't have to be anything fancy. I'm thinking something kind of remote, very rural. The view is very important to me, and I like water, ponds, rivers, things like that. Are there any creeks or streams around here?" he asked. Had to give it to him, that was pretty smart, considering the address was on Creekside Road.

"Well, there is one little road with a creek running alongside it. It's called Creekside Road. Isn't that clever?" she giggled, looking at me again in the mirror. I pretended I hadn't caught her comment. "Anyway, there aren't any houses for sale out there. And even if there were, you wouldn't want to live on Creekside. When the rains are heavy, the creek comes out of its banks. It can be kind of scary for the people who live along there. It's really isolated."

"Where exactly is that?" Russ inquired.

"Far side of town," she answered quickly. "But there's nothing for sale out there."

"What about property, acreage?" he asked. "Maybe something I could build on."

"Hmmm." She thought for a minute. "I'll check. I don't think so, but if there is I'll let you know. If you find a spot you like, I guess it's always possible to ask the owner if it could be purchased. Why don't you look around, let me know if you see anything? I'll be glad to contact the owner and ask for you." We were back at the motel, and the tour was over. At least we had a better idea where Creekside Road was.

"Well, thanks for your help," Russ smiled as we got out of the car. He turned, leaned into the car, and asked Cherilyn, "Would you have dinner with me tonight?"

"Well, yes, I suppose I could," she replied. "Steve, sure you don't want to meet my sister?" she asked.

"Oh, I'm sure, but thanks anyway," I said, mad as hell and beating a path to the door of the motel room. Russ stayed, finalizing arrangements for dinner. Michael was still passed out across the bed, and Jim was in the bathroom. I guessed it was his reading time. Seemed that's what I'd be doing later too.

"Great going, Steve. She thinks you're gay," Russ chuckled, dropping into a chair beside the bed. "And

I've got a date for tonight. You know, you could still see the sister."

"No thanks," I sighed. "I think I'll go to the convenience store for dinner. I think Jim needs to get out."

"How exciting," Russ commented, prowling through his suitcase for a clean shirt.

"Yes, it is," I responded, "especially if you remember that the convenience store is on the same end of town as Creekside Road."

"Ah, yes, so it is," Russ nodded. "Good luck."

"Thanks. I'm going to need it."

He'd found the note, scribbled on a dinner napkin and tucked into his rolled newspaper. "Meet me in the barn behind my house at eleven o'clock tonight. Don't tell anyone. I love you. Claire." The darkness was so thick he could hardly see the barn. A faint light flickered inside.

"Claire, you've got to tell me what's wrong. What is it?" Distraught and shaken, Bill stood helplessly as the tears slid down her face and into the handkerchief. "Please! I can't do anything unless you tell me what's wrong!"

"You can't do anything about this," she sobbed, sniffing loudly.

"How do you know? Maybe I can. I can at least try, can't I?" His plaintive tone calmed her somewhat, forced her to collect herself to tell him, to break the news somehow.

"You can't," she said, looking into the green eyes. "Unless you can find a way to become Jewish."

His brain began a slow spiral downward, darkness growing and dread slipping in. That was it, the monster with which he'd have to do battle. But how could he fix this? How could he fight this?

"We'll see each other. It'll be all right, I promise." He hugged her close, kissing her forehead. "We'll meet here, spend as much time together as possible. We'll find a way."

"What if they catch us, Bill?" she asked, eyes wide and sorrowful. "What will we do then?"

"We'll think of something. But I'm not ready to give up. Are you?" He waited, wondering what her answer would be, knowing the opposition she'd face if she continued to see him.

"No!" There was a firmness, a determination, in her voice. "Whatever it takes, no one will break us up. No one."

Long months of facing the enemy, surrounded by German tanks. Endless days in foxholes, eating food unfit for human consumption. Watching his buddies die, one by one, at the hands of a madman. None of that seemed as hard as this. That pain had been dulled by this girl and the wonder of her love. The pain that replaced it, this revelation, was greater than any he had ever known. This enemy, one he couldn't see, was bigger, stronger, and more hateful than anything that had come against him before.

chapter 6

I decided to walk to the convenience store. Big mistake. As I walked along, I noticed people staring at me out the windows of their houses and from their cars. That's when it hit me: They thought I was Native American. So much for being inconspicuous.

One thing I noticed, though, was that there was a bridge in the center of town, something I'd missed before. The water running underneath it was too small to be a river, but too large to be a drainage ditch. A creek. It ran behind the convenience store and continued on through the trees. Beside the convenience store was an intersection, and I had to wonder if the street turning off was Creekside Road. It didn't take long to get the answer. The clerk at the store was eager to talk, especially to someone he didn't know.

"Does this river out here have a name?" I asked, feigning ignorance.

"It's a creek," he corrected me, "and it's called Rocky Creek a-cause it's so rocky." Brilliant name. "It goes 'round behind the store here, and keeps on a-going.

There's some rapids down there somewhere, but it's really shallow and too narrow to boat. But it's pretty."

"I'd like to do a little hiking. Is there a trail, or a road, or something like that?" I asked innocently.

"Yep, there's a road. You just turn here, and then go right. That's Creekside Road." Bingo. "The road dead-ends 'bout three miles out. But it's pretty god-forsaken and lonely out there. Better know your way 'round good."

"Oh, I'm an experienced hiker," I assured him. "I'll be fine. Thanks for the information." It was all I needed to know. I couldn't wait to tell Russ what I'd found out when I got back to the motel.

But I had to wait. He was gone all night. Chalk one up for Russ, the first to score on the excursion. He turned up at about six the next morning, sneaking around like no one could hear him come in. Michael had been asleep since the afternoon before. I'd never realized how much he drank until that trip. I was awake, listening to Jim wheeze in his sleep. I got up, walked into the other room, and motioned for Russ to follow me out onto the porch.

"I know where Creekside Road is," I told him. "You want to be first to go? Are you going today?"

"Going today?" he snarled. "I've been up all damned night. I'm going to bed."

"Nice going," I snapped back. "I thought we came here to find Nick Roberts, not the Incredible Double-Jointed Woman."

"You're just jealous, you fag," he snorted at me caustically. "You could've spent the night with her sister if you hadn't talked yourself right out of it."

"Right, whatever. Are you going or not?" I asked again. I could feel my cheeks burning and my blood pressure rising.

"No way. I told you, I'm going to sleep. If Michael wakes up, I'm going to get him drunk again so he'll keep sleeping. Cherilyn and I have another date tonight, and I have to get my strength back before then. She's amazing, really. If her sister is anything like her, you're missing out," he grinned.

"Fine!" I was growing angrier by the minute. "I'll do it. I'll find Nick Roberts. I'll think with my big head instead of my little one, unlike anyone else in this group, and I'll find Roberts by myself!" I left a stunned Russ standing on the porch as I turned and marched back into the cottage.

I dressed in my standard hiking attire, comfortably-worn jeans, a tee-shirt, and a chambray shirt over the tee, sleeves rolled half-way up my forearms. I took the elastic off my hair, brushed it out good, fastened it up higher, and pulled the entire length of it through the opening in the back of my cap. Heavy socks and my hiking boots finished off the package, and I threw some stuff in one of the backpacks I'd brought along. A couple of bottles of water, a couple of granola bars, and a good clock/compass combination, as well as a flashlight, fit nicely into the pack. I added three bandanas, and another pair of socks, just in case I got into water, and threw in a plastic bag for trash and the possibility of wet socks. It was about half-past six when I brushed past Russ and locked the door behind me. As I passed him, I heard him say, "Good luck." It was the second time in less than twelve hours that he'd said that same phrase to me. He said something else under his breath, something about an "anal-retentive bastard," but I didn't care, didn't ask him to repeat himself.

I set off down the road, little clouds of dust puffing up each time a foot hit the ground. Looking up, I noticed some gray clouds drifting around on the horizon in the direction I would be going. Nothing big or frightening, just a haze. Just as well, since I'd forgotten my sunscreen. Within minutes I was turning at the convenience store. Up ahead, about two city blocks, the road ended, with a turn to the right or left. The sign to the left read "Tucker's Pass." There was no sign for the road to the right. It had to be Creekside Road. Turning right, I began to slow and enjoy the scenery. Only one house in sight, but on the mailbox in hand-painted black letters were the digits and words "2 Creekside Road." I was on the right track. The creek meandered along the edge of the road but, oddly enough, the house was on the other side of the creek, accessible only by a little wooden bridge that crossed the creek from the road to the driveway. The next house visible was a good mile away. Twenty minutes later, I was squarely in front of it, where a mailbox adorned with stick-on letters and numbers announced "5 Creekside Road." Didn't Russ say the address for Roberts was 19 Creekside Road? That would be at the end of the road, I guessed, or at least very close. I noted that the house I'd just passed was situated like the first, across a small wooden bridge from the road. I could see a little cluster of houses about another mile away. Knowing it would be a long hike, I took in the sights and sounds so different from my usual surroundings.

The houses were all to my right, as was the creek, gurgling and bubbling as it tripped across the rocks. The air was so quiet that even my footsteps seemed loud, cracking the silence and intruding like a marching band in a church service. Watching carefully, I saw a chipmunk and a squirrel, tails flicking, fighting at the base of a tree, probably over a long-lost nut now found. The field on my left was newly mown, the smell of the greenness almost overpowered by the masses of molasses-sweet honeysuckle along the fence row. Large round bales of hay dotted the landscape, and a lone cow stood near one, pulling stale-looking fodder off the outside while a small bird landed repeatedly on its back. It would stomp a front hoof and the bird would fly away, only to return in a moment. The cow stopped eating briefly and mooed, and from somewhere far across the pasture another cow returned its call. All kinds of birds were twittering and chirping nearby, birds whose songs I couldn't identify, but one, a mockingbird, sang a loud, purposeful cantata in a tree along the roadside. A small snake crossed the road and slipped down the creek bank. Someone's hunting dogs, a pair of beagles, ran along the other side of the creek, oblivious to me. Everything smelled old, like dirt and grass and wet rocks, with some grimy, spongy moss thrown in.

It had been years since I'd been in an area like this. Ever since I'd hired on at The Knoxville Advocate, I'd been trapped in glass, concrete, and steel. I liked the city, liked the way it hummed, the way it glowed in the dark. But I missed the wilds too. There was plenty of wide-open mountain country around Knoxville to enjoy, but I never seemed to have the time to check it out. Everyone talked about the wonders of Gatlinburg and Pigeon Forge, but I'd only been three times, and once was passing through on this trip. The other two times had been business, conferences I'd had to attend, meetings in which I was trapped for days, never going out into town and exploring, denied a chance to experience the hilly, green beauty I'd heard so much about. All that kept me from going insane was the view of the bluish-gray mountain foothills from my office window. Donna had begged me to take her to this cheesy little chalet village in the foothills, but I had always been too busy. Maybe the new boyfriend would give in, fulfill all her dreams, make her wishes come true.

I sighed, and a sensation hit me right in the chest, like one of those luminescent sticks being bent until the inside casing breaks, mixing the chemicals to make the plastic tube glow. It hurt, but it felt good. A sense of relief swept over me, and I felt my lip quiver ever so slightly. They did make sense, all those tree-huggers chaining themselves to tall timber. If this was the way they felt, being in touch with everything natural in the universe, I understood their stance.

The light breeze pushed me from behind, stroked my face as it parted against my back and then reconciled in front of me, making me its courtesan, including me as part of its own. That portion of me that had been quiet, almost dead, stirred and moaned, stretching as it woke from its long nap. The sun played hide and seek behind the puffy gray clouds, kissing spots along the road, creating glittery blips in the creek's ribbon of water. I watched the ripple of the flow, wondering where that water had been, if it had a story about a storm or a gentle spring shower, or maybe ice melt, from up high on some mountainside.

About that time I noticed that the road had gone from cracked, weathered blacktop to gravel. It looked like riverbed gravel, that reddish-brown, sandy mixture dredged up by whomever the Corps of Engineers contracts with when the channels get too shallow. A ridge cropped up in the middle, complete with weeds and grasses, while either side held tire ruts where repeated use had firmly packed the sandy mixture. My feet couldn't decide, the ridge or one of the ruts? I consciously chose a rut, tiring of the slap of seed heads against the legs of my jeans. Looking ahead, it became obvious that civilization was dwindling from the condition of the road. In several places the tire grooves were nearly washouts, and the span grew more and more narrow. I'd passed the three houses just a few minutes before, the last of which had been adorned with a "12" above the front door. Instead of sun, the road was now covered with overhanging tree limbs, filtering out the light, cave-like and cool. More weeds grew in the center on the ridge, which was now not as pronounced because of low traffic. Even though it was clear this portion wasn't traveled as much, it seemed to have been traversed recently. There were stripped and broken limbs above my head, small ones, where a vehicle seemed to have hit them as it came and went. The creek turned to the left, and so did the road, continuing to follow the creek bank.

I walked along for some distance, seeing only small patches of sunlight through the dense canopy. The road turned sharply to the right and, as it straightened out again, there was a mailbox on my left, across from which was another of the twenty-foot-long bridges spanning the creek. Plainly displayed on the mailbox were the markings, "19 Creekside Road," and the decorative painting on it looked very much like a patchwork quilt, clearly the work of a woman's hand. I stopped, looking at the tiny gravel and dirt drive. It traveled back about a hundred yards on a steep incline and disappeared over the crest of the hill. Nothing else. Not the top of a house, a barn, nothing was visible, just the drive which seemed to stop in midair and hang there, mocking me. With my excitement was a little apprehension. *So close and yet so far*, I thought, staring at the hill.

The road continued on, and a plan began to come together in my mind. There just couldn't be another house back here, I reasoned, and the condition of the gravel road surface gave credence to my assumption. It thought it might be best to hike to the end of the road and come up the back side of the hill, as if I were truly out on a recreational jaunt. The end of the road was very near, just a few hundred feet as it turned out, and it was plain to see what it was used for: A dump. There were old washers and dryers, an abandoned truck chassis, and something that looked a great deal like hair dryers from a beauty shop. An old bedspread and some ragged, half-rotted towels were thrown around. Springs sprouted from a decomposing sofa, its long deceased partner chair baking in a sunny spot a few feet away. Fortunately, nothing had been thrown in the creek, which I personally felt would have been a shame. I was sure that some-where farther downstream, some fish was truly grateful for the clean, clear water.

After I'd stared at the evidence of man's progress for a few seconds, I turned my attention to the water. Shallow spots seemed hard to find in this particular creek, but the water was clear enough to alert a wader to any underwater dangers that might exist. Finding no good place to cross, I decided to sit down and take stock for a minute before going on. I dropped my backpack and dug through it until I found a granola bar and one of the bottles of water. The breeze was stiff, and I cooled off slightly as I sat on the grass, my back against a tree trunk, staring at the creek. The rocks were down deep enough to be useless for crossing, but big enough to cause the rippling effect on the surface. It was a peaceful place, calm, unlike the features office. No phones ringing, no people asking questions, just a few birds, a noisy squirrel overhead, and some clouds. *A man could get used to this*, I mused, remembering pictures of log cabins and the sod huts built by sod-busters on the prairies. It almost sounded attractive. Almost.

When I finished the granola bar, I removed my shoes and socks, packing them in the top of my backpack. I rolled up the legs of my jeans as far as I could, which wasn't very far due to the fact that I wore them too tight and knew it, and waded in.

The water was cold, colder than I'd expected at that time of year. In just a matter of moments it was up to my knees, and I quickly realized that my jeans were going to get wet, no way around it. I looked for footing, and found I could maintain a depth of about mid-thigh high by moving from rock to rock below the surface. It took only about three minutes to cross carefully, primarily because the width of the creek had diminished somewhat at that spot. A large rock graced the bank, gray and inviting under a broad-leafed tree, and I dripped my way over to put my socks and shoes back on, but not before trying to squeeze the water out of my jeans. Pretty confident that I was alone, I took off my jeans and wrung the legs out. I found myself wishing I had on some plain cotton boxers, because I'd sure have felt foolish if someone had come along and seen me in the silly cartoon character printed boxers I'd packed for who-knows-what reason. The boulder bit into my backside as I perched on it to put the jeans back on. Their cold, clammy legs made it difficult to get my feet out, and I felt generally uncomfortable. To make matters worse, they made my socks damp. I almost forgot the excitement I'd felt when I'd seen the mailbox.

Picking up my backpack, I ran my arms through the straps and started up an incline behind me and to my right. That seemed to be the general direction of the driveway. The hill didn't seem too terribly steep until I was about halfway up. It was one of those gradual inclines, the kind that semi-tractor/trailer rigs struggle with in the mountains, and my legs, encased in the wet jeans, were getting heavier and heavier. To add to the problem, the tree cover was sparse, and the sun was getting hotter with each step. As I passed the halfway mark I stopped to catch my breath.

That was when I heard it. The music. Some kind of droning, stringed instrument, unidentifiable to me. I continued upward, stopping every few steps to make sure I was still moving in the direction of the music. After a few yards, I listened again and heard something I hadn't heard before. It was a voice, sweet and pure, not especially high, but definitely a woman's voice, singing with the strumming of the strings. I squatted down, my hands on the ground, and looked around. About sixty feet to my left, a clump of bushes perched at the top of the rise. I moved like a sidewinder across to them, ever so slowly, and peered through the branches.

I could see the driveway to my right, coming down the back of the hill, moving directly across my line of vision, and at its end, there was a house. It looked to be an old farmhouse, square and squat, probably built at the turn of the twentieth century. Its clapboards were a little warped, and it very nearly screamed for a coat of paint, its silvery patches gleaming in the sunlight. There was a tiny little screened-in porch on the front, and the low concrete steps sported a little calico cat, licking her paw and rubbing her face. A couple of huge trees framed the house from my vantage point. I could see sunflowers growing just to the left of the scene, and a washtub was turned upside down and leaning against the tree on the left. The music still wafted on the breeze, but the singing had stopped. Its direction was unclear, and my eyes darted back and forth until I found her. Then she began to sing again.

Almost hidden from view by the stand of sunflowers was a porch swing mounted on a frame, a homemade kind of frame made from rough timber and set in the ground with a post-hole digger. The frame stood under another tree, a medium-sized tree, which I believed from my distance to be a maple, and faced me. She moved forward and back ever so gently in the swing, with a box-like instrument the likes of which I'd never seen before perched on her lap. I wanted to get a closer look at its shape and strings, but I couldn't even see it for the woman. Too far away to make out her features, I was stunned by her hair, a coppery gold, more reddish than the sunflowers nearby, but still blond. More intriguing than the color was the glitter, almost like golden threads woven into it. I wondered if she had some kind of glittery preparation on it. I'd never seen anything like it. It was long, a good ten inches past her shoulders, and not curly but wildly wavy, wispy in the gentle breeze. She had on some kind of dress or jumper a shade of faded denim, with a printed long-sleeve blouse under it, and tan moccasin-type shoes with no socks. She was leaning over the instrument, fingering the strings with one hand, strumming with the other, and the effect was magical. I wondered if I should just come out from behind the bush and introduce myself, or if it would be better to move back toward the drive and come up that way. I backed out of the bushes and began descending somewhat, crouching as I went.

And then I did one of those things you pray you won't do at a time like that. I slipped. Maybe it was a slick spot in the grass, or maybe a loose rock, I don't know, but my right foot just disappeared from under me, followed by the left. I went down hard, face first, and the breath was knocked completely out of my chest. I'm not sure exactly what I did, but I made some kind of noise, probably a big grunting sound, like someone being struck in the stomach with a baseball bat. That would make sense, because that's precisely how it felt. It took a few seconds for me to get a grip on myself, and I lay still on the ground, a little afraid to move for fear I'd broken something. I moaned and groaned a little, softly, of course, and collected my thoughts. I managed to get my hands up even with my shoulders, palms down on the ground, and began to push myself up when I felt something cold and metallic against the back of my neck. A voice said in an authoritative tone, "Don't move." Then it dawned on me – there was a shotgun pressed into my brain stem. I froze.

"Don't move," the voice commanded again, and I felt a foot in the small of my back, pressing down. The voice belonged to a woman, and it was very strong and loud. She must have heard me and come around from behind while I was recuperating in the dirt.

"Don't worry, wouldn't think of it," I replied, still gasping for breath. It was my immediate assumption that I needed a brain stem to survive, that it was a necessity of life, and that a shot straight into the brain stem would kill a grown man. I didn't intend to find out, not if I could help it.

"Good," she barked. "Want to tell me what you're doing out here?"

"Hiking," I answered, spitting grass out of my mouth. "I don't think I'm hurt, but I'm really uncomfortable. And I'm having trouble breathing. I'm not going to hurt you, I swear, but could I please get up? Please?"

"No!" she retorted, an edge to her voice, grinding her foot harder into my back. Was she afraid? With a strange guy sneaking up on her? Probably. "I'm going to reach into your back pocket for your wallet. Don't move, okay? I don't want to hurt you."

I almost chuckled. "I don't want to be hurt either. Left side, I'm left handed," I instructed, helping her as much as she'd allow.

"What's your name?" she asked. I knew she was comparing what I said to what was in my wallet. I was really glad I'd removed my press pass.

"Steve. Steven Joseph Riley. I'm forty-eight. I'm six feet, one inch tall, and I have dark brown hair and brown eyes," I offered, knowing that was all on my driver's license.

"Yeah? What's your address?" she inquired teasingly.

"Ninety-eight fifty-four Westchester Drive in Knoxville. Ever heard of Knoxville?" I chided her. I wanted to turn around and look at her, but the gun barrel was still embedded in the back of my neck.

"No, wise ass, I've never heard of Knoxville. Why don't you give me a geography lesson?" she snarled, leaving me wondering how someone with hair so beautiful could be so nasty and caustic. *I bet she's got a wart on the end of her nose*, I thought. *A witch with a shotgun.* "Why are you really here?" she insisted, pressing the shotgun deeper into the base of my brain.

"I'm hiking. I like to hike. If you don't believe me, I'll show you my legs," I taunted. Maybe that high-priced health club would pay off after all.

"For a guy with a gun at the back of his head, you're real chipper," she quipped. I could hear some of the tension fading from her voice, and she took her foot out of my spine. That was a good sign.

"How 'bout you let me up? We can talk, I'll show you some pictures of my grandma, stuff like that. I think you'll like me. I'm not an axe murderer or anything like that," I joked, trying to reassure her.

"Get up then. But don't turn around until I tell you to," she barked. I could hear her backing away, but I was betting that gun was still pointed at me. I stood slowly and brushed the dirt off my shirt. "Okay," she said, "you can turn around slowly."

"Would you be more comfortable if I put my hands behind my head like on TV?" I asked, half serious, half joking.

"Whatever!" I could tell she was becoming irritated at my arrogant attitude. I clasped my hands behind my head and turned around cautiously. Taking one look, I couldn't help but begin laughing out loud.

She was standing, looking directly at me, feet about fifteen inches apart and planted firmly. That wild mane of blond hair was waving in the breeze, which had picked up somewhat, making the golden locks look very much like a halo around her head. Large, gunmetal blue, laughing eyes, complete with tiny lines at the corners, stared right into my face, one eyebrow raised quizzically. She was fair, a pale lavender tone residing directly under the surface of her soft, smooth skin, and her cheeks carried the rosy glow of someone with whom the mountain air agrees. She had a lusty, voluptuous shape, very soft and sweet, her dress draped over her short, round frame. I saw evidence of a body once very slight and willowy, evidence borne in the tiny wrists and ankles and slender, curvy legs.

But in her hands she held the source of my amusement, drooped at an angle in front of her. It was a piece of pipe about three feet long. The shotgun. Her mouth was curved into a lop-sided smile, and as I began to laugh, she started to chuckle. She broke into an open laugh as I blushed, a little embarrassed that a woman half my size with a pipe in her hand had kept me lying face-down in the dirt for what seemed like an eternity. Her eyes twinkled teasingly. Then I remembered I had my hands behind my head, and laughed a little harder as I pulled them down and brushed them on the sides of my jeans. She pressed the end of the pipe into the ground, leaning against it as she continued to snicker, and I stepped forward, right hand outstretched. Her grip was firm.

"Steve. Steve Riley. But I guess you already knew that," I smiled, looking straight into her eyes.

"Diana Frazier. Somewhat pleased to meet you," she replied, her smile revealing straight, white teeth. "Sorry. But one can't be too careful, you know."

"I understand completely. I'm sorry I scared you. I was just hiking and heard you singing. I wanted to find out where the sound was coming from and then, old stumble-bum here, I made a fool of myself," I explained, still blushing a little.

"I'll forgive you if you'll have some tea," she offered, surprising me slightly with her hospitality. "You've got dirt all over you. I hope you have something clean to wear."

"Well, not exactly," I admitted. "I hadn't anticipated this part of the ultimate hiking experience."

"You're wet too. Did you ford the creek?" she asked through squinted eyes.

"Yep. I ran out of road. It's no big deal, though," I said, stomping my feet to break the wet jeans legs free from my skin.

"Let's see what we can do about all this. Have you had anything to eat?"

I was really hungry. "No, not a thing," I lied, telling myself that a granola bar wouldn't count.

"I've got some chicken salad, bought it yesterday at Mac's," she offered. Apparently that was what the locals called the convenience store. "I have some cheese too, and some lettuce and tomatoes for salad. And I know I've got frozen stuff," she added.

"I don't want to impose. I kind of dropped in on you unexpectedly," I chuckled.

She smiled, a warmth in her eyes that I hadn't seen earlier. "That's okay," she said. "I don't get many visitors out here, so one every once in a while won't hurt me." She headed toward the house. I watched her go, hesitating, not sure if I should move or just watch her, her hips gently swaying under the dress, her hair sparkling in the sun.

"Well? Aren't you coming?" she asked as she turned, a puzzled expression furrowing the space between her brows. "Come on. The wind's picking up."

I grabbed my backpack and headed up the hill. She waited until I reached her and walked slowly beside me, looking at the ground as she moved toward the house. My anticipation grew. I was hoping, praying, that I was about to find out more about Nick Roberts, but it seemed unlikely. She seemed unlikely. At the top of the steps, the screen door pulled open easily with my bruised right hand. I half bowed and swept my left arm toward the opening, an exaggerated act of chivalry and courtesy.

She played along, curtsied, climbed the steps, took about five strides across the porch, and opened the front door. "Come on in," she invited, and I stepped across the threshold.

As Bill made room for the flour and sugar shipments on the store shelves, he thought about Claire. He thought about Claire constantly. She was his waking thought, the focus of his lunchtime musings, and the last thing he saw in his mind as he fell into a fitful sleep each night. He had begun to wonder if they would ever find a way around the taboos of her family's religious beliefs.

A voice jostled him out of his working reverie. "Boy, don't you have some flour around here?" He turned to see a stern, dark-haired man scowling at him.

"Yes, sir, we have Blue Bell, and Hickory Mill, and . . ."

"I'm looking for Kosher flour. There must be some here, but it appears you've done a good job of hiding it. I have to assume that's intentional."

"Oh, no, sir. It's right here." Bill reached for the bag on the top shelf, but the man blocked his arm.

"I'd rather you didn't touch my purchases any more than necessary," the man growled, spitefulness flowing through his words. "I'll get it myself." He snatched the bag off the shelf and, as he walked away, Bill heard him mumble, "Damn gentiles."

In all his life, Bill had never heard anyone say the word "gentile" with such hatred. He watched the man's back as he disappeared around the end of the aisle. Then he thought of Claire.

Is that what Jewish people went through every day in the gentile world? Were they made fun of, called names, ridiculed? He knew all too well what they'd gone through in Europe during the war – horrible atrocities, things no human should have to endure or witness. If he and Claire had a child – when he and Claire had a child – would their child have to endure callous words from people who didn't understand that only love was considered as his or her reason to be?

He'd have to ask Claire what her experiences were. It was unimaginable that anyone would talk to her, around her, about her, like that. She was sweetness and goodness and sunshine all wrapped into one beautiful gift, her lips the big red bow on the top. Nothing like that would ever touch her or their child. Bill would see to that. He'd protect them from the ugliness the world would throw at them. It was his duty.

His mind drifted to one of his favorite daydreams – a pregnant Claire, full and round with their child, a child made in their love and nurtured to be a great man or woman, someone who would bring hope and love into the world just by their goodness. That's who he'd raise their child to be, an honorable, trustworthy, gracious, compassionate human being regardless their ancestry, religious preference, or life situation. They'd then produce grandchildren for him and for Claire, modeled in their image, a force of positive emotions, and work to carry on their legacy. He and Claire would live on in them, and the world would be a better place because of their love.

chapter 7

"**S**houldn't you get something for me to sit on?" Loose dirt and dust were still all over my clothes, and I was trying to be polite. I hadn't expected the state of my cleanliness, or lack of, to be a problem from the looks of the house's exterior. Looks can definitely be deceiving.

"I've got a throw over there that you can use," she said and motioned across the room. I moved across to the brocade wing-back chair to pull the soft, dark green throw onto the seat, arranging it so that I sat only on it and not the chair itself. "I'll make you a sandwich. Here's your tea," she said, handing the frosty glass to me. Tea never tasted so good. Sitting in the chair, drinking the tea, I had an opportunity to really take in the room.

The chair I feared soiling was a dark burgundy and green fleur-de-lis, its legs a warm, rich mahogany. Its twin sat facing me across the hearth of the huge fireplace which was tiled with a warm, deep red, unglazed tile, its creamy grout lines perfectly aligned. The hearth sported a handsome set of brass firebox tools, the handles constructed of some type of faceted glass, ruby red and highly polished. The sofa facing the fireplace was pale eggshell with dark burgundy, blue, and green patterns, sparse but intricate, sprinkled all over it, and dark burgundy piping. The seating pieces were arranged around the edge of an enormous area rug. I'd seen them made on television, the pieces of carpeting carved and inlaid to make the pattern rather than painting or dying it in, and it was a work of art in itself. The artwork over the mantle was a classic pastoral scene, complete with children and horses, and the mantle was covered with smiling faces beaming from inside an assortment of classy frames, along with some carved and painted pillar candles of various shapes and sizes on various types of metal, glass, and wood holders. What I believed to be a huge coffee table was really a large ottoman, upholstered in a dark green brocade and sporting a custom-sized piece of tempered glass an inch thick as a top. The table itself was adorned with several books, beautiful art books and a special edition on the meaning of various types of flowers, along with a large volume of Shakespearean plays and a pictorial volume featuring cathedrals in America. A variety of occasional tables, a sofa table, and various other pieces completed the room, including massive bookshelves on either side of the fireplace, and all held fine treasures, pieces of what I recognized as expensive porcelains, fine china pieces on display stands, and statuary. The walls were painted a dark, peaceful blue like that of the figures on the sofa, and the creamy woodwork matched the sofa print perfectly. It was, well, regal, extremely classy and well-appointed. And there was no television, I noted with curiousity, at least not that I could see. The entire room was open into the kitchen. She spoke to me, but I wasn't paying attention.

"Preoccupied?" she quipped.

"A little," I said, trying not to seem embarrassed. "I'm afraid I'll get your furniture dirty."

"I suppose you're a little surprised," she commented, sawing with a knife blade at whatever culinary offering she was creating. "I'm sure it's got to be a little shocking. I mean, I know the outside of the house doesn't look like much, so people seem taken aback when they see the inside. But I like it. It's comfortable – it's home."

"It's beautiful," I almost gushed. "I guess I expected it to be sort of plain."

"Like me?" she smiled, not looking up, a hint of sadness in her question.

"Not at all," I responded quickly. "I just thought that the outside of the house seemed plain, so I suppose that's why I expected the same kind of interior." I wondered if the same surprising opulence held true for its owner, and I wanted to change the subject. "So what is it that you do, Diana?"

"I'm an artist," she answered, tossing the salad while she spoke. "I work with textiles, mostly fabric, yarns, threads, things like that. I don't sew, but I do weave." She hesitated for a moment and added, "I sculpt too. I like plaster, concrete, wire, metals, things like that. No painting, not like painting pictures or drawing or things like that. But I do like to do decorative finishes. My favorite is concrete. I like working with it. But that's not how I make my living. I make hand-crocheted rag rugs the way my grandmother taught me and sell them over the Internet. They bring a good price, and it pays the bills. I guess that makes me an arts and crafts whore, huh?"

"I wouldn't say that," I responded. I wasn't getting the answers I wanted, but I didn't want to rush things. She came toward me carrying a tray, which she placed on the glass-topped ottoman. It held a beautiful plate dressed with a pickle spear and some fresh fruit, a chicken salad sandwich complete with cheese, and the accompanying bowl held a crispy salad, garnished with wedges of tomatoes. She returned with a similar tray for herself, but on it she had included about five different kinds of salad dressing, some napkins, and salt and pepper in exquisite ruby cut-glass shakers. "Help yourself," she said, motioning to the dressing. I chose a balsamic vinaigrette, complete with Parmesan cheese. The first bite was heaven. I hadn't realized how hungry I was. She watched as I ate, a tiny smile at the corners of her mouth, seeming pleased that I was enjoying it.

"Throw many of these dinner parties, do you?" I asked, my mouth half full.

"Nope," she responded, not looking at me again, staring down at her plate. "None." She didn't add anything, and made no further comments. I tried again.

"Lots of pictures on your mantle," I stated, gesturing in a sweeping motion with my finger. "You're in some of them. Friends?"

"Mostly family," she mumbled. Again, quiet.

"Do they live around here?" I was getting nowhere.

"No."

There was a wedding band, wide and flat with three or four stones, on her left ring finger. "So, did your husband help you decorate this place? It's a lot for one person," I blurted out. In a flash I was sorry I'd done so. She seemed to shrink before my eyes, her shoulders droop ever so slightly, her face grow pale. There was a misty, far-away look in her eyes, eyes that suddenly looked old, tired, bluer than blue. After a few minutes, she spoke.

"My husband's dead," she stated with quiet clarity. "So are my children." She'd stopped chewing now, and I noticed that the sun had stopped shining both inside the house and out. The wind had picked up considerably, but there in front of the fireplace, the air was still and thick. "Accident at work. The doctors said it happened so quickly that he never felt a thing." She stopped, collecting her words and thoughts. "I was pregnant three times. My first son died two weeks before he was born – a weird heart disorder. My daughter died of sudden infant death syndrome when she was four months old. When I was pregnant with the second boy, we had a car accident and I miscarried. So after my husband died, I moved here to start over. But that was a while ago."

"I'm sorry," I stammered, embarrassed and ashamed of my rudeness, my insensitivity. But how could I have known? I tried to recover and move forward. "Aren't you afraid to be out here by yourself?"

"Well, no," she snapped indignantly, a bit put out at my inference. "Coyotes and wolves don't rob a person, and I've never seen a deer take out a gun and shoot anyone. I'm safer out here than I'd be in a city." From the things our reporters told me they'd seen and heard on the streets, that was the truth.

She brightened suddenly and set her tray on the coffee table. "Want some more tea? There's plenty."

"Sure," I said, glad she'd broken the heavy spell that had fallen on the room. She returned to the kitchen and I rose, placing my tray on the coffee table across from hers. I stood in front of the fireplace, admiring the smiling faces in the pictures. There was a very young Diana looking out of one gilded frame, smiling and waving at the camera. Next to it was a picture of her and an older woman, probably her mother. In a tiny copper frame was a photo of a newborn baby – her daughter, I presumed. A little farther down the expanse was a beautiful wooden frame, inlaid with pieces of mother-of-pearl in bell shapes. Inside the frame a couple smiled for the camera, dressed in wedding attire. That was him, Nick Roberts, I guessed. They looked happy, satisfied with their choice of partner. It all seemed crystal clear now.

If I had to guess the whole story, I'd assume she sold his book after he'd died. He wouldn't have been the first person who was more successful in death than in life. She lived comfortably here in a house she'd purchased to start over, licking her wounds and bandaging her soul with art and music. She'd said her last name was Frazier, which was bound to be her family name. Our trip was a bust. Nick Roberts was dead. The only thing left to do was to find out where his grave was and tell the world, for what it was worth.

She returned with my tea. "Like the pictures?" she asked, smiling.

"Yes, very much," I answered. I pointed to the one of her waving. "Nice shot."

"Um-hum," she hummed, sipping tea at the same time. "That was David's favorite photo of me. And that's me and David on our wedding day. He was a great catch."

She'd called him David. Maybe that was his middle name or a pen name. I'd have to find a way to ask, but right now it was more important to keep up the rapport. I turned to comment on her hairstyle in the photo when a flash of lightning caught my eye, followed by a deafening crack of thunder. A noise I was unfamiliar with filled the house, and I must have looked alarmed. She giggled.

"Rain," she said. "This house still has a tin roof. Sounds funny the first time you hear it, doesn't it?"

"Sure does," I replied, still a bit startled. "Guess I'd better be starting back."

"Oh, no, you can't walk in a storm like this in the mountains," she said, that authoritative tone creeping back into her voice. "One of the most dangerous lightning strike places to be in the whole world, the mountains. I'll drive you into town."

"I really don't want you to go to any . . ." I started, but she shushed me.

"No trouble at all. Let me get an umbrella and bring the car up here, though," she offered, reaching into an umbrella stand near the front door. At that moment an enormous bolt of lightning struck somewhere nearby, and the power flickered twice, then went out. I flew to the window and looked out. Rain was coming down in sheets, so heavy that I couldn't see the car in the drive.

"I don't think we're going anywhere," I said resignedly. She put the umbrella back in the stand and picked up the phone on the table next to the door. I could tell by the look on her face that it was dead as she slowly put it back in the charging cradle. It was getting dark, and I knew that if it didn't let up soon, I'd be stuck there. That would be truly awkward.

"Okay, let's see. I have a gas water heater, so there's plenty of hot water. How 'bout you take a shower while I soak your clothes on the back porch?" At that moment, the power snapped back on, but the rain didn't let up a bit. "And if the power holds out, I can wash and dry them too. At least you'll be clean when you get back to, where did your license say you were from?" she pivoted, realizing she knew little about me.

"Oh, three of my friends and I are staying at the Blue Bell Inn," I explained, "because Russ, one of the guys, is being transferred to a company near here and he's looking for a place to live. I like to hike, so I used his trip as an opportunity to get some hiking in. Great excuse, huh?" I smiled.

"Sure, and a free trip too," she laughed. I heard her footsteps fade down the hallway on the other side of the kitchen, and she returned with a large, dark green terry cloth robe, her initials monogrammed into the lapel. "Here, put this on and get out of those filthy jeans," she ordered, pointing toward the hallway. "Go into the bedroom and around the bed to get to the bathroom. If you'll put your clothes outside the door once you take them off, I'll get started on them." Buckets of rain poured down the windows. I had to admit, I had nothing better to do. I meandered down the hall, robe in hand, past several prints of wild flowers. I tried the doorknob at the end of the hall on the right. It was locked.

"Wrong door," she called out. "The one on the left."

Her bedroom wasn't as stately as the living area in the front. Lace curtains graced the windows, and a lace coverlet lay draped over the seafoam green comforter. The walls were a pale, cool shade of lavender, and held several art posters tastefully framed. One was a Monet, and one was an enhanced reproduction of the photo from the cover of *Midnight in the Garden of Good and Evil*. Both had gallery names along their lower borders. There was a soft floral arrangement in a Longaberger basket on the dresser atop a hand-crocheted runner.

The bathroom echoed the same decor, complete with glycerin soaps, dried flowers and leaves embedded in them. I hung the robe on the back of the door and peeled out of my jeans and shirts, careful not to leave clumps of caked dirt on the floor. Once I'd stripped out of every piece of clothing I'd been wearing and wrapped them all in on themselves to contain the mess, I laid them carefully outside the bathroom door and called,

"Okay, my clothes are outside," down the hall. Then I locked the bathroom door, wondering if I were about to reenact a night at the Bates Motel. But I had to admit, the hot water was wonderful, and I never knew soap could feel so good.

Then I remembered that I'd put my underwear out there too. Oh, well, I was pretty sure she'd seen a guy's underwear before, but then I remembered I'd been wearing the boxers with the cartoon characters on them. Wonder what she'd think about those? The thought made me laugh. The lights flickered a couple of times but stayed on. I could still hear the rain pounding on the roof, a deafening sound, even above the rush of the water from the showerhead. The water pressure changed abruptly, then returned to full force in a few minutes. Assuming it was the washer kicking in, I knew she'd started on my clothes. There was no turning back now. I hoped the power held out.

The gardenia-scented shampoo and conditioner rinsed out of my hair easily, and I turned the water off and stood for a second. Her towels were pale lavender and huge, and they carried the scent of lilac, like an old lady on Sunday morning. I'd never touched a towel so soft. Once I'd dried off, I put on the robe. It came right to my knees, and was roomy, warm, and comfortable. Opening the bathroom door, I looked and, sure enough, my clothes were gone. In their place was a pair of boxers, never worn. I picked them up, stepped back inside the bathroom, and slipped them on discreetly under the robe. That seemed pretty strange to me. She answered the question in less than a minute.

"Guess you're wondering about the underpants, huh?" she laughed.

"Well, as a matter of fact, yes," I admitted as I headed back down the hall to the living area. She was nestled in a corner of the sofa, feet up and in snugly socks. She held a cup of steaming tea in her hands.

"Bought them to sleep in and they were packaged wrong, wouldn't fit. But I kept them. I don't know why." Then she grinned. "Someone knew you would need them," she explained to us both. "Tea? I love it when the weather's bad. Want some?"

"Sure. But don't get up. I can get it myself." I reached for a cup and saucer sitting on the counter. The whole kitchen was tiled with the glazed version of the fireplace tiles. It was impressive, immaculate, and very inviting.

"So," she started, "Mister Steve Riley, tell me some things about you. You've been asking all the questions. What about you? What do you do for a living?"

"I'm a writer," I said, then corrected myself. "I mean, I'm a journalist. I write for the Knoxville paper. I'm a feature writer there. Before that, I worked for a regional magazine, some small weekly papers, things like that. Then I hit the big time, at least I suppose that's what you'd call it."

"Um-hum," she acknowledged, sipping her tea. "Never met a real writer before." I wanted to scream,

What about Nick Roberts?, but I held my tongue. She pushed on. "Where's your wife?"

"Don't have one," I said in a flat tone. "Never had one. Don't particularly want one, either." She looked a little startled.

"They tell me everyone wants someone to love them," she smiled. "Don't tell me you're not included in that 'everyone.'"

"I had someone who loved me. Problem was, she loved lots of other guys too," I spat, thinking about Donna and my doctor bill. "I have a career, a nice home, a nice car. I can get a date when I want one."

"You mean you can get laid when you want to, don't you?" she snapped, instantly lifting the tea cup to her lips to hide the mischievous smirk on her face.

"Yeah, I guess that's exactly what I mean," I shot back. "What's wrong with that?"

"Gee, I don't remember," she answered me, feigning an unconcerned demeanor as she set down her tea cup. "It's been six years for me."

Oops. I couldn't begin to imagine where this conversation was heading, but I could hear the train wreck it would cause a mile away. Then I caught what she'd said. Six years.

"Wow. That's a long time," I mumbled. "Six years. That's a very long time." I repeated myself, trying to imagine not being with a woman for six years. I couldn't. It just wasn't possible.

"Not really," she mused. "I was married to the same man for almost sixteen years. I know when you fall off the horse you're supposed to get right back on, but I just haven't been able to. But then you wouldn't understand, now would you?" She looked out at me from under her bangs and brows, a teasing grin curling the corners of her mouth.

"No, guess not." I couldn't imagine being with the same woman for that many years. This question and answer session had not gone as I'd imagined. I looked out the window but it was inky black, so dark that there was nothing to see except the reflective sheets of rain pouring down the glass, interrupted by little bits of dirt or bird droppings stuck to the panes. She noticed that I was checking out the elements, and she rose and opened the front door.

"Listen," she instructed. All I could hear was the sound of the rain on the roof. I shrugged. She said it again: "Listen."

I could hear something, but I didn't recognize the sound. "What's that sound?" I asked.

"It's the creek. It's rising. Ever heard of a flash flood?" she asked in a solemn tone.

"Yes, I have," I answered, apprehension in my voice.

"That's the sound you're hearing. The creek's out of its banks. But don't worry, we won't be flooded up here. It's just that it floods the bridge. You'll probably need to stay here tonight." I shuddered. Staying in a strange house with a woman I barely knew who hadn't had sex in six years sounded a little frightening to me, but it was better than drowning or being swept away. "You can sleep on the couch. I'll get you a blanket, some sheets and pillows, things like that. You'll be fine." Whew. I'd escaped the sequel to Planet of the Nymphomaniacs. Or perhaps I should think of it as a great opportunity. Nah, surely not.

She motioned for me to return to the living area, and she turned to follow me. Then she stopped stock still and whispered emphatically again, "Listen."

I heard it. It was a creaking, rubbing sound, and I could feel the hair on the back of my neck bristle, as though someone were scraping a chalk board. "What is that?" I asked. Before she could answer, there was a strange crash, like a dozen trees falling in a forest, only very close by and very muffled. It was followed by a rushing roar which quickly faded, and then just the sound of the rain on the roof again. I looked at her, questioning with my eyes, and noticed that her face had gone pale and her hands had begun to tremble. "What was that?" I demanded, hoping to snap her out of her stupor, to get an answer.

Her eyes were moist, and I panicked, afraid she might cry. "That was my bridge. It's gone." The words sunk in like lead in my stomach as the rain beat down, pummeling the earth, the house, everything everywhere, while the rain-swollen creek received it all. Pregnant with the deluge, it had given birth to a catastrophe. But we were dry, and we were indeed safe.

And there we'd stay.

Bill straightened his tie and slicked back his hair one more time. He glanced in the rearview mirror of the old Buick. His father had warned him to expect nothing, but he was hopeful. Better yet, Claire had no idea he was coming to see her parents, specifically her father, and she'd be surprised to see how well it went. Even with his injury, he could present himself well, and he knew it.

The doorbell rang, loud enough that Bill could hear it on the porch, and the door opened. A young girl not more than twelve asked, "Can I help you, sir?"

"I'd very much like to speak to Mr. and Mrs. Steinmetz if I may," Bill announced, very careful to speak formally and correctly. Their first impression of him was important, he was sure.

"Let me get them," the girl offered. She disappeared, leaving the inner door open, and Bill could hear her relaying his request to someone inside.

A dark shape moved through the interior light and toward the door. When it reached the door, a voice asked, "How can I help you?"

Bill took a good, long look and blinked. He knew this face and voice from somewhere, but where? And then it hit him.

The rude man at the store. God help him, it was Mr. Steinmetz.

It was a fight to keep from stuttering and stammering, but Bill tried his best. "Mr. Steinmetz, my name is Bill McInnes. I wanted to come by and introduce myself to . . ."

The man's face contorted in disgust. "You've got no business here. I've already told Claire she's not to see you. Get off my property."

Bill decided he'd go the hardline route. He'd been a soldier, for god's sake. "Mr. Steinmetz, Claire is an adult. She can see whomever she pleases. I'd just like for it to be a positive thing, not a situation where she feels condemned by her family."

"I'll tell you what's condemned by her family – a filthy gentile, and a crippled one at that. You'll not see my daughter. You'll not come near my family."

"Mr. Steinmetz, I fought in the war to protect the people who share your ancestry. I would think that would be a plus for me, would it not?"

Mr. Steinmetz's face was red with rage. "You think the fact that you got paid to traipse around Europe with a gun and kill people you didn't even know should afford you a seat at my family's table? My daughter is a Jewish lady, you Scotch-Irish trash. She'll marry a decent Jewish boy and that's the end of it. Now leave before I call the authorities and have you arrested for trespassing."

Bill looked down and shook his head. "I'm sorry you feel that way, Mr. Steinmetz, because I love your daughter. No one could take better care of her than I could, and no one could love her more than I do. I hope you'll reconsider."

"When Hitler comes back to life. Now go. And don't come back." With that, Mr. Steinmetz slammed the door in Bill's face, and Bill was left alone on the porch in the dark. He had met the enemy, and he didn't have a single weapon to fight with except his heart.

chapter 8

The sofa was pretty comfortable as sofas go. Diana gave me a flashlight, just in case the power went out. She also showed me the powder room just inside the hallway entrance. It had no shower or tub, which explained why she didn't ask me to clean up in there. By the time she'd made my sleeping arrangements for the night, my clothes were in the dryer. We were making some progress, even if things looked bleak outside.

I lay awake, looking at the ceiling for a long time. I'd thought I was in Nick Roberts' house, but it appeared I was wrong. Most likely Russ had bad information. I guess they were wondering about me by now, or maybe not. It was a sure thing Russ was doing the horizontal Macarena with Cherilyn the Wonder Lay, and Michael was drunk out of his mind. That left poor Jim but, hey, he's a grownup. Maybe it was time he faced a crisis on his own. It might help him toughen up.

The sound of the rain on the metal roof was almost deafening, meaning it was still pouring. I thought again about Nick Roberts. Why would someone write something so powerful, so meaningful, and then hide? I remembered the parts of the story I'd liked best. There were many good points, but just a couple that had really taken up residence in my memory.

The first one had to be when Claire's father, Arnold, had paid Bill to disappear. I didn't think Bill would go, but he did. Roberts' description of Claire's shoes, worn and dusty from walking back and forth to work after she sold her car to pay the private detective, was writing at its finest. Those shoes had taken on a life of their own, virtually breathing and telling the story themselves. I'd hated her father for what he'd done, for the pain he'd caused her, for being so controlling and judgmental.

But the most important part, the one I'd liked most, was also the one that was the most painful, the most tormenting. It was after Claire had moved to the city, when Bill saw her on the trolley. He'd cried out to her, but the noise of the street crowds was so loud that she couldn't hear him. He'd called and called, tried to push his way through the crowd, but he couldn't. He could see her, almost reach out and touch her hand, screamed until he was hoarse, but she hadn't turned around, hadn't heard his cries, hadn't seen his anguish. The trolley had zipped away, and he'd been left in the crowd, pressed into a sea of people but very much alone, his heart broken. He stood there and watched the trolley move away, holding the flowers he'd ripped from the hands of a little boy, blinded by his pain and the consequences of his decision.

Thinking about the book, my chest ached. I'd lived with four women and very nearly married the last one. In between, I'd dated and slept with dozens, beautiful women, prestigious women, wealthy women. Unlike Donna, some of them had been totally faithful to me but, for one reason or another, I'd lost interest, wandered away, or been given the brush-off.

Dominique had been one of the better ones, raven-haired and busty, a golden island girl, but when she got the offer to teach in New York, I'd refused to go. I missed her body, but I'd tired of the endless fitness routines, bottles of vitamins and dietary supplements, and the beauty regimens that changed weekly.

Margaret was definitely the most intelligent woman I'd ever known, but her intellect emasculated me. I was afraid of her, afraid of disappearing into marvelous mental Margaret, of having no identity of my own. That's how housewives feel, I'd always imagined. We went to wine tastings and gallery openings, and everyone noticed Margaret first. I wasn't used to that. In the end, she got tired of begging me to have a life, and she left.

Katherine, on the other hand, was completely different. She'd been loyal, warm, and a great cook. A country girl at heart, she liked natural things, like herbal tea remedies and those funny wrinkly skirts. I even managed to tolerate her potions and spell-casting rituals, but her natural birth control methods scared the hell out of me. Every month was a nightmare of "Am I pregnant?" and it wore on my nerves until I locked up like an Edsel with a hole in the oil pan. She came home one day from her job as a massage therapist and I'd packed all the bottles, jars, and boxes in crates and put them outside the door. She came in during the weekend while I was at a workshop and picked up the rest of her things. I never laid eyes on her again.

But Donna, she'd been the epitome of womanhood for me. Smart, sexy, funny, self-sufficient, she'd kept my motor purring from the first time I met her at Jill and Marty's wedding reception. She had on this clingy blue dress – I can still see it in my mind – and her legs were longer and finer than any I could've possibly dreamed of. They'd wrapped around my waist tight and fast that first night, and stayed there almost constantly over the next year. I'd discovered away from the bed that she had a great sense of humor, was a successful architect, and treated me like more man than one woman could handle. For the first time in my life, I felt complete, like I had everything I could possibly ever want or need. I'd taken my Christmas bonus and bought the biggest honkin' diamond I could afford. The plan was to take a trip to San Juan in June and get married there. We would take a cruise, and I'd propose on the ship. Then, when we made land, we would tie the knot and honeymoon the rest of the trip.

But sometime during February I spent the night in her apartment – she wouldn't get rid of it – while mine was being painted and she was out of town. When I came in from work, there was a strange message on her answering machine from someone named Paula, with this poor woman crying into the phone and begging

Donna to leave her husband alone. At first, I'd passed it off as a misunderstanding, but I didn't say anything to her about it. Then I started noticing other unusual things, like flowers in her office that weren't from me, or expensive gifts with no cards attached. She always had an explanation until the night I came back early from an interview and found an unfamiliar car in her driveway. I let myself in and discovered she'd gotten to know my old college buddy, Frank, a lot more intimately than I'd ever known him. That was May. I took a woman I'd only been out with twice to San Juan, banged her all the way there and back, and never called her again. Just thinking about the whole thing made my throat tighten and my eyes sting.

What must it be like for Diana? Fifteen plus years with the same guy. I'd always heard married sex was better than any other, but I never could figure that out, how two people never got tired of each other. More than that, they had shared their lives. She had to be lonely, going from a couple to one person in the snap of her fingers. Even though she was alone, she seemed happy enough. She'd been playing that instrument and singing when I'd come upon the house. There had been this peaceful, serene look about her, something I'd seen in few people. If there was a secret to that serenity, I hoped she'd share it with me. I could use it. I tried to remember the tune she was singing and playing, something lilting. It had reminded me of an Irish tune, or maybe Scottish. I remembered how her hair looked in the sun it seemed we'd never see again.

He lay awake, thinking of — who else? — Claire. She'd become the center of his world. Sure, there'd been others, but they had been of no consequence.

There was Elizabeth. She'd been his mother's choice, all red hair and pale skin and big, luminous, blue eyes, as Irish as they came. They'd gone to elementary, and then junior high and high school together. Everyone thought they'd marry, but Elizabeth had other plans. The night he caught her with the Callahan boy from down the street, her dress up around her waist and leg wrapped around his bare ass, Bill had walked away and never looked back. No one understood. He refused to ruin her reputation in the neighborhood, but she certainly would ruin his in a marriage.

And then there had been Consuela. He'd been attracted by her exotic darkness and big brown eyes, not to mention her huge breasts and tiny waist. She'd been the one to take his innocence, and what a taking it was. Every other girl after Consuela had commented on what an accomplished lover Bill was, and he had the dark-skinned beauty to thank for that. His mother had hated her until she found out the girl was Catholic; then she could walk on water and turn it to wine. But when Bill announced his intentions to join the military, Consuela had decided she didn't want to be tied to someone who might never come back, and that was the end of the long, passionate nights in the little room behind the cantina her parents ran.

And of course, Greta — ah, Greta had been a charmer. He'd found her in a brothel on a back alley in Lyon on his way to Lourdes during a rare break from duty before he was sent to combat. His mother had begged him to go to the Sanctuary of Our

Lady of Lourdes and bring her back a small bottle of the healing water from there. He'd tried, but the bottle had gotten broken in a fire fight and he'd never made it back there to get more. But Greta had made him glad he'd stopped in Lyon, and he'd made it a point to stop there on the way back as well. She'd been an experienced entertainer of men for quite some time, even though she was barely twenty, and the nights he spent with her were exquisite. She'd charged him for the first time, but after that, she looked forward to being with him and slept with him for free. He'd never forget the night she'd brought in two more of her friends and they'd spent their time pleasuring him. But he had to get back to his duty station, and then the fighting began. That was the end of that, and he never saw Greta again.

But Claire — Claire was different. She was goodness and purity, and he wanted to bury his manhood in that purity and never come up for air. Just holding her hand did things for him that none of the other women he'd known had been able to do. Her fervor for life was contagious. And he wanted to lose himself in that fervor, to be the reason for at least a part of it. If they could hang on, he'd see to it.

chapter 9

The roar of the rain took a backseat to the smell of something baking in the oven. I blinked a couple of times and looked at my watch: Nine-thirty in the morning. I'd slept fitfully once I managed to actually get to sleep. I could hear Diana rustling around in the kitchen, and the sound of water running through the coffee maker. Life was good.

"Morning, sleepyhead! Rest well?" She looked exactly like she did the night before, hair soft around her face and a pink floral gown and robe wrapped around her. A plate of freshly-baked sweet rolls sat on the table, plates already out and fruit bowls filled. She had a coffee cup ready, and I took it, gulping down a big mouthful of the steamy, fragrant elixir before even trying to speak.

"Aaaaahhh," I sighed. "Yes, as a matter of fact, I did. That sound the rain makes on the roof is a great sleeping aid. You should record that, patent it, and sell it!" I smiled as she chuckled, pleased that I could make her laugh so easily.

"Well, at least your clothes are clean now," she reminded me. "That's a plus."

"And the power held out," I interjected, trying to remain cheerful at the prospect of being trapped in the house.

"Right. But the phone's dead and so is the cell service," she frowned. "I think that first lightning bolt must have done it in for good. There's no way to call anyone, but in this rain there's nothing they could do for us anyway. In a day or two, when the rain stops and the mail carrier comes down here, he'll discover the bridge out and we'll get some help. In the meantime, I have plenty of food for both of us. We won't starve."

"Entertaining ourselves might be a problem," I commented, wondering what we'd do for the next few days.

"I've got books and magazines, even if they are old," she replied. "And we can play board games or card games, or tell stories – you're a journalist, for god's sake. I can get out my Tennessee music box and play, and we can sing." So that's what that thing was. I'd research it when I got home but, for now, I didn't want to seem ignorant.

I reached down and rubbed my knee. Pulling up the hem of the robe, I saw that it was kind of swollen from the fall. Diana noticed me looking at it and rounded the end of the counter just in time to see.

"Oh my gosh! Does it hurt?" she gushed, bending over it to get a closer look. Her hair fell down around her face, and as it moved its fragrance was released, a scent so soft and sweet I wanted to bury my face in it and breathe like a man coming up for air.

"Not much. I don't think there's anything really wrong with it, just some bruising." I bent and flexed it, noting that it didn't so much hurt as it ached.

"Go sit on the sofa and I'll get you an ice pack. If I'd known last night, we would've already done this." Little sergeant that she was, she herded me to the sofa. She grabbed my ankles as I sat down, and hoisted them up so I was turned sideways with both legs elevated. Then she scurried back to the kitchen and returned with a zipper seal bag filled with ice and wrapped in a dish towel. "This should help get the swelling down." Sitting on the floor beside me, she tucked both ends of the towel under my leg to keep the pack in place. Without even thinking, I reached out and stroked her hair.

She gasped instantly, and I drew my hand back. My startled, embarrassed expression must have registered immediately with her, because her fiery glare changed to a soft, confused look in a split second. "My god, I'm sorry," I stammered, still holding my hand against my chest as though it had been burned. "I don't know what just happened here. I wasn't thinking. I didn't mean to do that, I swear."

Her voice was soft, almost quivering. "That's okay. It has that effect on people," she tried to explain. "Complete strangers sometimes ask me if they can touch it. I don't mind, really." I could tell she was trying to put me at ease. I felt my heartbeat beginning to slow and my cheeks began to cool.

"Really, I don't know why I did that," I repeated, trying to explain something for which there seemed to be no explanation.

"I told you, it's okay," she almost whispered. She put her hand on mine and patted it lightly, a reassuring gesture. "It's been a long time since anyone's touched it." Her eyes were soft and smiling, and I wanted to touch her again, to stroke her cheek.

"Do you mind?" I asked, a sense of wonderment growing, not understanding what was happening, but liking it.

"Absolutely not. Go ahead. David used to play in it all the time, braid it and brush it and such, but there's no one to do that anymore." There was an edge of anguish in her voice, and my hand instinctively reached out, my fingers touching the golden strands lightly at first, then brushing through it, stroking the tender skin beneath it as I drew it through my fingers. She leaned sideways against the couch, her arm bent and resting on the cushion palm down, her face resting on her forearm, eyes closed. She sighed. I wondered what was going through her mind. Was she remembering? Could she remember? How long had it been since someone had held her hand, or wiped a smudge of mustard from her chin, or hugged her hello or goodbye? I leaned up a little, wanting to see the expression on her face. It was blank, expressionless, except for a tiny tear, clear and perfect, rolling like a pearl out of the corner of her eye, down the side of her nose, and across the top of her upper lip. I thought about the studies I'd read in psychology class, how children who received no attention or affection withered and withdrew after a while. I didn't pity her. Instead, my heart broke for her, for lost dreams and silent evenings, for rooms full of belongings she'd parted with, each box more heartbreaking than the one before. What kind of pain made a living, breathing member of the human race choose to isolate themselves so completely?

After a few minutes, I realized she was asleep. The tear had dried, and she was completely still, breathing slowly and noiselessly. I managed to pull my legs up against my chest and turn on the sofa so as not to disturb her. Once my feet were back on the floor I stood, bent down, and scooped her up. For her size and shape, she was surprisingly light and, strangely enough, she didn't wake. I carried her back to her bedroom. The bed hadn't yet been made, and I put her down lightly. I watched her breasts rise and fall with her breathing, and then drew the sheet and blanket over her. She snuggled into the pillow, and I pushed the magic golden locks back from her face. Her cheeks were as rosy as her lips, and she sighed. Her mouth moved the tiniest little bit, and I wondered if she were talking to someone in her dream. I smoothed her hair one more time and turned to leave the room. In her dream state she whispered almost inaudibly, "I love you." For some unknown reason it seemed the right thing to do, so I bent over her and whispered in her ear, "I love you too." I brushed my lips against her cheek, and she smiled that sleeping smile, the smile of a small child napping for the promise of ice cream. The door closed without a sound behind me, and I stood in the hall for a minute, leaning against the smooth coolness of the door, wondering what had just happened. I thought about Bill, about the book. I thought about the sleeping woman on the other side of the door, probably dreaming about a happiness she might never have again.

And what about me? What was waiting back home for me? I had nothing, no one. I had a job, a career, but no one to ask about my day when I came through the door. No one was glad to see me unless I had my column ready. We weren't so different. Our paths to these points in our lives had been different, but the destination had been pretty much the same.

I reached across the hall and tried the knob of the other room. It was locked up tight. What was in there? Where were all these questions coming from, and why did I even care? My mind was a jumble, with Bill and Diana and Claire and Russ and everything I knew and did spinning in wild arcs, maddening and incomprehensible.

It was definitely time for another cup of coffee.

"Bill, this will never work. I can't make you hang on for something that will never exist. Please, please, go and have a happy life." Claire was weeping, her shoulders convulsing with sobs. "I had to lie and say I was going to the movies with Leah just to be able to talk to you. And if she tells, I'll never hear the end of it."

"But it will work, sweetheart. Just have faith, please? I'll find a way to make it work." Bill stroked her velvety cheek and sighed. "Perhaps you should try to find work so you can move out."

"Oh, no! That would be the wrong thing to do. A single Jewish girl moving away from home to work and live? My family would put the kibosh on that pretty quick." She sniffled and wiped her nose with a delicate embroidered handkerchief.

"Then what? What can we do? There's got to be a way." Bill had thought and thought about it, but he was coming up blank. Her family's ideas were so different from those with which he'd grown up that he really didn't know which direction to take.

"I don't know. But I'm desperate to find a way. I love you, Bill. I want to be with you, have a life with you." Her eyes were still glistening with tears. "Do you love me?"

"Does the sun rise in the east and set in the west?" He smoothed her hair and looked into her eyes. "Of course. Always."

chapⴀⵦⴀR 10

While she slept, I checked out the house a bit. I noticed a fairly old computer in the dining room at the back of the house, and I flipped it on, thinking perhaps I could send an e-mail to a friend to let someone know where I was. Then I remembered; the phone lines were down, and she sure as hell didn't have cable. Strangely enough, it wasn't plugged into the phone line anyway, and there was no software for e-mail or the Internet showing up on the desktop or in any of the directories. I remembered she'd said she did business on the Internet. How exactly did she do it? I backed out of the programs I'd opened and shut it down.

There was a coat closet right inside the front door, but it yielded nothing of interest except a couple of board games. One was an ancient Yahtzee game, and I opened the box. Inside, old scorecards were jumbled up and scattered, some with childish handwriting. I held one up. At the bottom, it said in tiny penciled letters, "Cindy's cheating!" It felt funny, holding something written by someone else so long ago, her sister or brother probably. But I had to chuckle. I could see them, sitting around a kitchen table sort of like on *The Wonder Years*, playing Yahtzee, her and her parents, her sister, and one of the kids yelling, "No fair, Mom! That's cheating!" It made me wonder, what would a child of mine look like? Dark, like me? Tall? Short? At the rate I was going, I'd never know. I put the lid back on the box and tucked it back into the cramped closet.

Drifting past the window seat, I looked at the raindrops hitting the glass panes. But I stopped, turned back, and flipped the lid to the window seat open, curious to see what it held. Small, flat shirt boxes, the type wrapped in red and green paper at Christmastime, were stacked neatly inside. On top of one was a greeting card, the edges of its flap yellowed and a little tattered. I slid the card out gently. The front, covered with a pastel floral pattern, said in pink foiled letters, "To My Wife on Mother's Day." The same typeface inside the card read, "For all you do, For all of those you love, For ever and ever, Happy Mother's Day." On the left-hand side of the interior were hand-penned words:

Dear Diana,

Words can't describe what you mean to me. I can't remember a time when I didn't love you and you didn't love me. I'm thankful for every moment we've had together, and I'm looking forward to growing old with you (not the old part, but the being with you part!). Thanks for everything you've done for me and tried to give me over the years. I'll love you forever.

Yours eternally,
David

Tried to give him – he meant the children. A dizziness came over me, and I realized I was holding my breath, making time stand still. My eyes welled with tears, and I quickly slipped the card back in its envelope.

I pulled the top box out and carefully removed the lid. Yellowed tissue paper concealed the contents, and I placed the box on the dining room table, pulling back the paper from each side to examine the treasures.

It was a tiny outfit, a white dress with the tiniest pink rosebuds, and a narrow pink bow at the neck between the sides of the rounded, lace-trimmed collar. The little ruffled panties underneath it were lined with rubbery plastic and carried the same rosebud design as the dress. With them was a pair of tiny socks, white nylon cuffed socks with pink lace sewn delicately around the edge of the cuff. In the bottom of the box was a tiny gold ring with a long length of the same narrow pink ribbon tied to it, just like the neckline bow. I pulled out another box, and found it held a pair of miniature blue jeans, a little elastic belt, and a tiny crewneck tee-shirt on which was emblazoned "Daddy's Boy." Lying flat inside the same box were a pair of size one high-topped tennis shoes, Nikes, their little shoelaces tied neatly, and a pair of baby-sized athletic socks, complete with red stripes around the calves. Her babies' clothes. There had to be a dozen boxes, but I didn't pull out another one. I wrapped the little garments as I'd found them and placed them back in the boxes, taking care to make everything look exactly as it was before, with the card on top of the boxes.

There was a sudden, sharp pain in my gut, the pain of a woman who'd never held two of her children, and had only been able to cuddle and love a third for less than six months. It was a horror I couldn't even imagine. Guilt swept over me, and my chest ached. I couldn't snoop anymore. I decided if I needed to know anything else, I'd just ask. Knowing what had happened to her family made the sacredness of her belongings too intense, too personal. I dropped onto the sofa and picked up a couple of the pictorial books, thumbing through and reading the captions. That kept me busy for a while.

It was close to noon before she stirred. I heard sounds coming from the end of the hallway and tiptoed to the door, listening carefully. She was in the shower. For reasons I couldn't explain, I wanted to sneak in and peek, just to see what she looked like under those heavy, unimaginative clothes. I fought off the impulse and went back to the kitchen.

When she wandered into the kitchen in an enormous polo shirt and a pair of jeans, she found me in a flowered apron, spatula in hand. She was completely surprised to see me in that role, I could tell. I'd found some hamburger patties and buns in the freezer on the back porch, and had oil heating in a deep skillet for the French fries. The shiny green tea kettle was working on a full rolling boil too, and I'd sliced tomatoes and washed lettuce for the burgers. A full range of condiments was displayed on the countertop, and there were plates, napkins, and flatware standing ready.

"Good nap?" I asked, breaking into a grin.

"Really good nap," she yawned, stretching a little. "I had a wonderful dream."

"Want to talk about it?" I gave her an opening, but she wouldn't bite.

"No. Think I'll keep this one to myself."

"Hungry?"

"Sure. Smells good. I didn't know you knew anything about a kitchen," she said with a winsome smile.

"A little. I'm no culinary whiz, but I can cook a mean burger," I quipped, flipping one of the patties and catching it on the spatula. She laughed and clapped her hands. She looked happy, rested. I hoped I'd played at least a minor role in the perkiness.

"Listen to that. The rain's slowed some. Maybe after lunch we can walk down the drive, see how much damage there is," she suggested. It sounded like an excellent idea to me. "By the way," she asked, head down, staring at the counter, "how did I get back in the bed? The last thing I remember was sitting on the floor beside the sofa."

"Me. You fell asleep, and I carried you into the bedroom." I didn't look at her. I was afraid to meet her eyes.

"Thanks. You can be a real decent guy when you put your mind to it. What's for lunch?"

"Burgers and fries. Real American fare," I said, dipping the golden fries out of the hot oil and placing them on a paper towel-lined platter to drain. "Healthy, artery-clogging stuff. Kind of like the stuff at the diner!"

She laughed and started dressing out her burger. We ate at the table in the breakfast bar in the kitchen, and we chatted away about the weather, our cars, appliances, mostly inane, safe things. She helped me clean up, and she chattered and laughed while I told stupid jokes I'd received via e-mail from friends.

When the kitchen was clean, she offered to show me the rugs she made, and I asked her to show me her technique. She did a couple of rows, and asked if I wanted to try it. I could see her frustration at my left-handedness, and she sat me facing her on the floor, legs folded Indian-style and knees touching, but not before she had gotten another rug she'd already started and handed it to me. She took a couple of stitches, and I tried it in a mirror-like fashion. She stitched, and I struggled. She laughed, and I laughed. After we'd fought with it for awhile, she pulled out a deck of cards, and we played and laughed most of the afternoon away. When I suggested strip poker, she frowned, then laughed, then made a goofy face. I took that as a no.

About four-ish, I suggested we check out the end of the drive, which she agreed was a good idea. I put my shoes on, ready to go. The rain was soft and quiet, not noisy as it had been the night before. It was steady, though, and it kept coming. At this rate it would take weeks for the creek to subside. I walked out onto the front porch, with Diana right behind me in her faded polo shirt and jeans.

"Want an umbrella?" she asked, reaching for an old, tattered one beside the door.

"Nah," I replied, knowing a little rain wouldn't hurt me. "I'll take my chances. We won't be out there that long."

"Okay," she responded cheerfully, and she went out the door without one too. At the bottom of the steps she waited for me, just like the day before, and walked alongside me up the hill toward the crest. I was anxious to see what had happened.

She had been right. The bridge was nowhere to be found. One pier remained on the other side of the creek. Everything else was gone, washed downstream like a handful of twigs in a storm sewer. We turned and went back to the house. As we walked back up the drive, I noticed that the shades were pulled down in the window which would have belonged to the locked room.

Back inside, she took the bath towel she'd used earlier and toweled her hair lightly, then tossed it to me. I took the elastic band out of my hair and did the same. I could feel her watching me, and I turned to meet her gaze. "What?" I queried.

"Why don't you leave your hair loose?" she asked me, her head cocked to the side as if to inspect it, to see if she approved. "It's really nice." I dropped the elastic and shook my head. Several strands fell down the front of my shoulders, and I could feel the rest hanging down my back.

"Better?" I asked.

"Yes, better." She smiled her approval. I knew women liked it for some reason, but I was never really sure why. As far as I could tell, she'd been completely honest with me about everything she'd said. I decided I'd just ask.

"Why do women like long hair on guys?" She seemed surprised that I'd asked, and reflected for a minute before she answered.

"Because, well, I think it has something to do with sensitivity," she responded slowly. "For some reason, women believe that a man with long hair must be more sensitive."

"That leads me to another question," I continued. "Why do women think writers and painters are more sensitive?"

"I guess their ability to express themselves," she reasoned. "Think about it. It's nice to be around a man who can express his feelings, especially in words."

"Even if they're bullshit?" I teased, watching her grin.

"Yep, even if they're bullshit. We just want guys to communicate, that's all." She kind of nodded her head, as though she'd just passed judgment on an important court case and knew she was right on the money. I chuckled.

"So where's the rest of your family? Parents, siblings? Are they back in your hometown?" I asked, looking to move the conversation in a different direction and get myself off the hook.

"Yes, they're still there," she answered politely, not looking at me. She sounded mildly irritated with the shift in subject. "I moved away to start over after the accident. Too many memories there, too many people pitying me, patting me on the arm, saying, 'Oh, honey, it'll get better, it just takes time.' I got sick of that. I couldn't heal. So I moved here because David and I had always loved this area; we'd been here a couple of times. My parents thought it was too soon. They said I was just running from the pain, that I wouldn't face it and deal with it. They won't speak to me because I moved away and left my husband and kids behind. But they're not there anymore, just a couple of rocks with their names on them, that's all. I really don't have anyone." She stopped, swallowed hard, and acted busy with the clean dishes in the dishwasher, leaving me to fish for another entry into her life.

"And your ancestry? Irish? Scottish? You're so fair and blond, maybe Swedish?" I guessed, waiting for her to respond. She put the plates she'd been holding down on the counter, wiped her hands, and leaned against the counter of the snack bar, elbows down and chin resting on her hands.

"Actually, Scot-Irish and German on my mother's side, British and Swedish on my dad's side of the family. Good guesses on your part." That explained her strength and determination. "And you? You're not a WASP, that's for sure," she smiled, that devilish twinkle back in her eye.

"No, no WASP here," I confirmed with a grin. "Well, the Riley side of my family was mostly Irish. But what you see here is Spanish. My grandfather was a dock worker in Bilboa. My father got a job teaching English at *Escuela Técnica Superior de Ingenieria de Bilbao*. He had an attack of appendicitis and they took him to the hospital. It just happened that my mom worked there, and he wound up on her floor for his recovery. He claimed it was love at first sight. That wasn't her story, though. She said he pestered and harassed her until she finally went out with him." I took a biscotti from the jar on the counter and snapped it in half before taking a bite. "It took him three years to convince her to marry him and come back to the states. They'd been here for about two years when I was born. By that time, Mom was working on her citizenship, and Dad was teaching at the University of Arizona. I don't have any brothers or sisters. How about you?" I asked.

"Well, I had one sister, but she died. Freak accident; she was sitting in an ice cream shop with some friends. Car ran a stop light, jumped the curb, and slammed into the building. She was killed; one of the friends with her has been paralyzed ever since. So I don't have any brothers or sisters. A bunch of cousins, but no brothers or sisters. My mom was one of six children, and her parents were from big families, so she always thought she'd have a big family too. But it was just me and my sister, and she was twenty when she died. She was the pretty one, the popular one. They were crushed when she was gone. They made it clear they wished that, if it had to happen, it had happened to me. They should've been more careful, though. You know, I'm all that's left to take care of them in their old age." She smirked, and then her face returned to its serious state. "But with the way they've treated me, I don't really have anything to do with them. I'm not sure I'll even know when they're gone, and no one will call me and tell me. Are your parents still living?"

This time it was my turn to swallow hard. Mom's death had been very hard on me, watching her suffer for months and months, unable to help her when all of the treatments had been exhausted. "No," I answered quietly. "They're both gone. Dad died in nineteen ninety-one, and Mom a couple of years ago. So when you get right down to it, I don't have anyone either."

She smiled and nodded. It looked as if we had more in common than I'd originally thought. I handed her the other half of the biscotti, and she took it, chewing thoughtfully and staring into space. The conversation had turned morbid, and I looked for a way to jazz it up quickly. "Got any old pictures? I love old pictures," I said, chewing again.

"Oh, yeah, bunches. Hang on," she called as she darted down the hallway. I heard a door open, then close. A couple of minutes passed, and the door opened and closed again. She brought out a box of old instant pictures, some yellowed studio prints, even tin-types. There were some old postcards too, and she laughed and explained the outing each picture represented. Some of them were pretty funny, and there were quite a number of pictures of kids, mostly cousins, but none of her. Not one. When I couldn't stand it anymore, I asked her, "So, where were you in all these pictures?"

"Oh, I'm not in these," she stated matter-of-factly, shuffling through more photos.

"Do you have any of you when you were little?" I asked insistently, determined to see at least one or two.

"Well, yes," she answered in a patronizing tone. "Hang on just a minute."

If I leaned out a bit I could see down the hall. The door I'd heard open and close was the one I'd found locked. I still wondered what was in there. Probably stuff that had belonged to her husband, especially since she kept old pictures in there. It was storage, had to be. I leaned out again, and noticed her coming out of the room, pulling the door closed behind her. But this time she didn't lock it, probably because she thought she'd take the pictures back soon.

They were all contained in a small box, like the shoe-box in which a toddler's shoes would be packaged. She opened the lid carefully and took out a yellowed four-by-six studio shot, probably a proof. A baby, just old enough to sit up by herself, looked into the camera with a happy, startled look. Her lips were pursed together as if to squeal or whistle, and her eyes were open wide, a sparkle glinting in the camera lens. She had dark, curly hair, and was holding the hem of her dress in her hand, most likely about to stick it in her mouth. "That's me. Eight months old," she said wistfully.

"You were adorable," I whispered, mesmerized by the look in the baby's eyes.

"Things change, don't they?" she mumbled. My cheeks suddenly felt warm, and indignation swelled inside me, surprising me, causing me to speak when I should have kept my mouth shut, I was sure.

"Not that much. You're very attractive. Not cute like a baby, but very attractive," I blurted out, wishing instantly that I could take it back, that I'd never said the words.

She was silent, still as a stone. It seemed like an eternity before she moved or spoke, and her lips moved softly, almost imperceptibly. "Thanks," she said. "I think you're beautiful."

I almost fell off my stool, didn't know what to say. A feature writer with no words, that was definitely something new. I'd been called lots of things, "handsome," "good-looking," even "hunky," which I personally thought was a little vulgar. One of my old girlfriends had called me "studly"; I liked that one best. But no one had ever told me that I was beautiful. I'd never even thought of a word like that being attached to me. Before I could collect my thoughts and say something, anything, the wrong thing, she picked up the little box and walked back down the hall, silent all the while. What the heck was I supposed to say now? I leaned out and looked. Sure enough, she didn't lock the door when she left the room. She walked back into the kitchen and simply said, "Want some dinner?" She never missed a beat. I was in the clear.

She fixed a grilled chicken salad and some breadsticks. Halfway through the meal, she gasped and sat up straight. "Oh, I almost forgot!" she exclaimed, and hopped up from the stool. She moved quickly across the room and opened a door I'd seen and questioned in my mind. I heard heavy footsteps, some shuffling sounds, and then more clunky footsteps. Stairs, I realized. It was some type of cellar.

"Homemade blackberry wine!" she announced, obviously proud of herself. "Can you grab those glasses over there?" she asked, pointing at a rack on the wall above the microwave. I pulled two stems down and wiped them with a checkered towel I found on the counter. She struggled with the cap, finally managing to peel the wax away from the edges and get the stopper out. The bottle was handed to me, and I ceremoniously poured both glasses full.

"To a new friendship," I toasted, lifting my glass toward hers.

"To a new friendship," she returned, and our glasses touched, a soft musical tone in the otherwise quiet house. The wine was good, sweet and robust with an earthy, dark fragrance. It had a kick too, and I told myself there couldn't be too much of that.

The rain was still coming down steadily, but not as hard as before. Things were looking up a bit weatherwise. It had grown dark, and we'd cleaned up the kitchen from dinner. We agreed to drink no more wine, but to save it for the next day. I wondered how we'd pass the evening. She answered the question for me.

"You're a writer. I suppose you read as well," she chided playfully as we sat down on the sofa.

"Well, yes, I like to read. I read as much as possible," which I'd have to admit wasn't much anymore.

"Do you like to read aloud?" she asked.

I was puzzled. "I don't mind," I replied. "Why? Do you have something you'd like me to read?"

"As a matter of fact," she said, her vocal volume rising as she headed back down the hall, "I have something here I'd love to have you read to me. That is, if you don't mind." She disappeared into the room again.

"Absolutely," I called after her. She held a small, hardcover book in her hands.

"Here. Read this. Maybe you've heard of it?" she quizzed, grinning ever so slightly as she sat down on my left. I turned it over and examined the cover. *The Grapes of Wrath*. I'd read it in college. I opened the front cover, and caught the mirth in her eyes when she saw my reaction: It bore an inscription from James Steinbeck himself on the fly page, and it was a first edition. "I got it through an online auction," she explained, stroking the cover. "Fifty dollars. The idiot who sold it didn't know what he had." Her voice seemed reverent, humble. *A strange purchase for a woman who makes rugs*, I told myself.

"It's easily worth one hundred times that," I stammered, wishing it were mine. I opened it to the first page, then stopped. "Ever read *The Celtic Fan*?" I questioned, watching her face for a reaction.

There was no hint of recognition in answer. "No, can't say that I have." I decided right then to just forget about Nick Roberts, and started to read.

After about five or six pages, I noticed she wasn't making a sound and hadn't moved in several minutes. I stopped abruptly and turned to look at her. The light from the table lamp threw a golden glow on her skin, and her hair cascaded around her face in tiny wispy strands, casting pale, wavy shadows on her cheeks. Her lips were parted slightly, and her eyes were trained on me, waiting expectantly, begging me to go on. She was hungry for the sound of a human voice, to know she wasn't alone, to feel connected. I knew that feeling well. It clung to me at times too, gnawing and cold.

Unplanned, unthinking, I reached toward her and stroked her cheek. She bent her head downward, her eyes gazing up at me from under their lashes. With no hesitation, I leaned forward and kissed her. I expected her to gasp and pull away, or at least react in some fashion, but instead she seemed to have anticipated it. I felt her lean in too and begin to move toward me. She rested her hands on my shoulders, on either side of my neck, and her fingers traveled upward underneath my hair, around to the back of my head, pulling me closer. Any anxiety, any apprehension or uncertainty I felt began to melt away as she moved up against me. She pulled her legs up and across mine, and I wrapped my left arm around her waist, pulling her tighter against me. Her soft, warm lips opened as I pressed mine against them, and I kissed her long and deep, trying to draw her into me, begging her not to turn me loose or turn me away. Running a finger down the left side of my neck, she continued around my collarbone and down the center of my chest, across my ribs, and rested her hand lightly on the top of the waistband of my jeans. I found my hands pulling on the tail of her shirt, pulling it up, wandering underneath it, up her back. Her skin was warm and soft, and she trembled slightly as I stroked her. The sound of my heartbeat pounded in my ears, and I pulled back long enough to look into her eyes. There was no sign of fear in the crystal blue depths, just warmth mixed with a little playfulness. I smiled and, placing a palm on either side of her face, I bent her head down, kissing her on the forehead, and she instinctively rested her cheek on my shoulder. With both arms wrapped tightly around her waist, I held her close, feeling her breathe into my neck. Her left hand lay gently on my chest, and I could feel her heart beating against my ribcage. I knew she was strong, that she could take care of herself, and yet I wanted to protect her, shield her from the rain, from the world, even from me.

"It's been six years, Diana," I whispered into her hair. I struggled, my mind trying to collect the words I needed to say, to say them the right way, to mean them when I said them. "Do you really want me to be the one? Are you sure it should be me? Are you really ready?" I held my breath, waiting for her to speak, to decide, to either shut the door or open it wide.

"Steve Riley, I don't think you have any idea what kind of man you really are," she replied in a soft, sultry murmur. She kissed the side of my neck, and then she asked the ten-million-dollar question. "Why not you?"

A million and one reasons raced through my head. My terrible track record with women. My ego, my arrogance. The way I delighted in displaying my verility. The fact that I didn't live here, didn't think I ever would, or even could. My inability to make a commitment. My unwillingness to hurt or disappoint this woman, this warm, open, strong, gentle loner, by walking out the door when the rain went away and leaving her alone again, golden and fair, singing in the sunshine. But the most important reason I could think of was the way I'd feel once I'd touched her, shared her bed. This was not a woman with whom you just had sex and walked away; this was a woman a man had made love to for fifteen years, a man who had loved her deeply for time and eternity. I was the one who wasn't sure I was ready, and it took me completely by surprise. I couldn't move, couldn't breathe, couldn't think. Reasoning and logic seemed stupid, and all that really mattered, everything important in my world, hinged on what I did in this instant. It was Diana who made the decision for me, who gave me a moment in time that will stay with me until my dying day. Reaching for my right hand, she placed it gently but firmly above her left breast, and held it there with a warm, velvety hand. I could feel her heart throbbing, almost hear its rhythm.

"You're already in here, Steve Riley," she said calmly, her voice as light and soft as angel's wings. "But where am I?" Her eyes searched my face, looking for an indication of my inclination, any clue of how I'd respond.

With a trembling lower lip and a shaking left hand, I took her hand off mine and held it tightly, palm down, against my chest just below my left collarbone. I knew she could see my heart pounding even before she felt it. I looked into those eyes and realized I'd entered into the first commitment I'd ever made. She stood and, in one fluid motion, removed her wedding band. She pressed it hard into my palm and closed my fingers tightly around it, holding my hand firmly closed. I pulled her to me and kissed her again, but this time it was different. This time it was with every fiber in my body, every cell, every drop of blood, every ounce of energy and passion I could muster. She pulled away, took my hand, and led me down the hallway toward the bedroom.

And I knew, really knew, we were both sure that it was right.

"But Bill, it's the only way! If I'm with child, they'll have to let us be together."

Bill was adamant. "No! I don't want your reputation besmirched so we can be together. If we can't do it right, we shouldn't do it at all." He gave her a disapproving stare that made her smile back, and then he couldn't help but laugh. "You have the strangest effect on me, Miss Steinmetz, do you know that?"

"I hope so!" She giggled and kissed him, just a soft, shy kiss. For a girl who was proposing an illegitimate pregnancy, she was surprisingly timid and naïve.

"Don't misunderstand me, Claire. I want you; I really, really do want you. But I really don't want our intimate relationship to start by trying to make a child for the wrong reasons. Surely you can understand that." He pulled her hand to his lips and kissed her knuckles.

She looked down and frowned. "Yes, I can understand that. It wouldn't be ideal for my first time, but . . ."

Bill's eyes went wide. "You're a virgin?"

She huffed. "Well, of course! I'm a good Jewish girl. I don't go around having relations with just anybody who comes along."

"That's not what I meant." Bill's blush was evidence of his embarrassment. "I just meant I was sure you'd had at least one relationship in the past, someone you loved, with whom you'd gone that distance."

"No, Bill McInnes. That privilege will be all yours." She leaned in and kissed him, and he couldn't fight it anymore. He cupped the back of her head in his hand and forced his tongue into her mouth, searching around, tempting, testing, and she met his every foray with her own gusto. It was a kiss that made the ground under their feet shake.

"Oh, no, red isn't your color!" she laughed when she finally broke the kiss, wiping her lipstick from his lips. "Bill, if that's a sign of your abilities, I want to go farther."

"I can hardly wait," he whispered, wrapping his arms around her waist and drawing her into his body. He could feel her hardened nipples against his chest through her thin dress and slip, and his hands longed to touch them, cup her breasts, kiss her soft belly, stroke her warm thigh. Every part of him longed for every part of her. Perhaps soon his longing could be satisfied – but only temporarily. He would want her again and again. He just knew it. And he'd want her to take his name.

chapter 11

I remember every second, every touch, every sigh, every moan of that night, every one. Time just stood still for us. I'd been a little concerned because I hadn't exactly packed a box of condoms in my backpack, but she just laughed. "They don't work as birth control anyway. That's how I got pregnant the second time," she'd giggled. "And I haven't been with anyone for six years so, if you're sure you're safe, I guess there's not a lot to worry about." I'd been tested since I'd last been with someone, about three months prior, so I was confident that things were okay in the STI department. And for some unknown reason, the pregnancy concept didn't really worry me either. I made up my mind on the long trip down the short hallway that I'd take this relationship as it came and be thankful for every minute I had with her. It only took a few of those minutes for me to realize just how thankful I'd be.

From the very beginning, there was no modesty, no shame, no embarrassment. As I undressed her she helped me, then she undressed me easily. She was more open than any woman I'd ever been with, asking what I liked, asking what felt good, telling me exactly what she wanted. The candlelight was forgiving, she told me, since gravity was not her friend, but I never saw anything I didn't love about her. Lying on my right side beside her, I took a good look, which she encouraged. I'd never seen nipples as large as hers, and she'd explained that apparently I'd never been with a woman who'd nursed a child. I had to admit not only that her guess was correct, but that it excited me a little to think about her nursing a baby, her own warm mother's milk nourishing a child. She just smiled and pulled my head down to her breast, where I teased her left nipple to erectness while I tweaked the other with my fingers. She moved a pillow under her shoulder blades so that her breasts looked like two mountains, twin peaks, and I was the mountaineer, scaling the slopes, conquering them, coaxing them to firmness and fullness, listening to her soft groans.

After a few minutes, my left hand moved down her soft stomach to a warm, waiting haven. Without coaxing or coaching, she opened her legs wide, unafraid. One worry was definitely over; she was completely and totally ready for me. I stroked her, watching her back arch and her hips thrust in rhythm with my hand while she begged me to go slower, to torment her, to make her want me more. Her hands wandered to my nipples, and she toyed with first one and then the other, moving down my stomach, finding what she wanted most. She was getting closer to her own paradise, her hand gripping me tightly, moving up and down my length with purpose, in rhythm with my own hand still moving on her. She moaned and bore down, I imagined as though giving birth, then shuddered and cried out.

Before I could reposition myself, she placed a hand firmly in the middle of my chest and pushed me to the bed. "Your turn!" she grinned, that mischievous sparkle in her eyes. Thinking she couldn't possibly mean what I hoped she meant, she kissed me hard and deep, then pulled her tongue out of my mouth and ran it down my neck. She mouthed each nipple, nipping with her teeth, and traveled farther downward.

"Are you really . . ." I started, thinking how many times I'd begged women for it. This couldn't be happening. I had to be imagining it.

"Wouldn't pass it up for the world," she spoke into my thigh, up which she proceeded to run her tongue until she reached a double impasse.

"One question," I mused aloud. "Are you a 'spitter' or a 'swallower?'"

"What do you think?" she laughed, licking up the column and surrounding me quickly and totally. I have to admit that, after my question had been answered, it was the first time in my life I'd ever begged a woman to stop anything done to me naked. She quit only after she'd helped me recover my density, and she dropped beside me on the bed, pulling me to her, kissing me deep, the taste of my gift to her transferred into my mouth, salty and thick.

Never in my life had I moved inside a woman the way I moved inside her. We didn't come up for air until

I'd "passed on my heritage" three or four times, as my grandpa would have said, and we were both exhausted. To my delight, she talked freely the entire time, about how she felt and how I felt to her, asking me what I wanted her to do and what I wanted to do to her, telling me what she needed. When I asked if I could just look at her, she chuckled and said, "Need a flashlight?" And then she produced one, which I did actually use, feeling like a miner in deepest, darkest Africa, joyfully exploring a new gold mine. She was perfect, accessible, and tight. I pulled her to me and she lay against me, on my right side and in my arms, her face resting on my chest, my hand teasing her right nipple, her pinching my left one.

"Feel like taking an adventure?" she asked, raising up on her elbow and looking me in the eye.

"Sure," I replied quickly, wondering what she had in mind.

"Come on!" she bubbled with excitement and took my hand. She headed out the bedroom door with me in tow, wondering what on earth she had in mind. On the way past the sofa she grabbed the throw and headed for the back door. I didn't know where we were going, but I didn't care as long as we were going there together.

The rain had stopped, a thing I'd noticed about an hour earlier during a "break." The moon was barely peeking out from behind a cloud, and the sky was layered with dirty, murky-looking thunderheads, but there wasn't a drop of rain. I'd noticed a swing hanging from a big tree limb, high enough off the ground that her feet wouldn't touch the grass below. It was a board swing, about three inches thick, two feet wide, and almost a foot deep front to back. She tossed the throw over the wooden seat and ordered, "Help me up." I picked her up and placed her firmly in the middle of the seat, grabbing a nipple with my teeth as I lifted her, listening to her giggle and shriek. She pulled her knees up to her chest one at a time and stuck her toes through the rope yokes on either side of the seat with one hand, like barefoot sandals on a hot summer day, and hung on with the other. I was still confused, until she parted her knees. She was completely open. Totally. And at just the right height. She got high marks in the sexual creativity department. I'd call her an erotic genius.

"Did you plan this?" I'd asked her, curious to see what she'd say.

"Of course not. I just thought about it a few minutes ago," she'd snorted, then reached out and positioned what I had to offer exactly where she wanted it. I dug my fingers into the soft flesh of her sweet ass and pulled her onto me. By pushing her back and pulling her forward I could go deep inside her with almost no effort, and she leaned back in the swing, her breasts heaving. About that time, a question came to me. I have no idea where it came from, but it just came out.

"What does it feel like to you when I'm doing this?" I asked innocently, stopping for a moment to wait for my answer.

"Let me show you," she offered, and took one of my hands. Placing it on her abdomen and pushing down firmly, she said, "Stroke."

I did. To my surprise, I could feel myself moving inside her. "What is that?" I puzzled.

"That's my uterus," she smiled. "You're moving it every time you push into me."

The next question came from nowhere as well, and shocked me right down to the socks I wasn't wearing. "Is that what it feels like when there's a baby in there? I mean, if someone puts their hand on your stomach when you're pregnant and the baby kicks, is that what it feels like to them?" I could hear myself asking and still couldn't believe the words were coming out. I felt like a high school kid in family living class.

She smiled, a smile of wisdom and years. "That's exactly what it feels like," she answered simply. No chiding, no giggling, and no question about what I was thinking or why I'd asked. She just answered my question. I continued to probe inside her with my hand on her stomach, marveling at the sensation. We moved together there, her in the swing under the cloudy sky, for a long, long time. I didn't want it to end, to stop. I wanted to be there forever. It didn't matter that neither of us were reaching any kind of climax or having any kind of earth-shattering experience. It was just comfortable, but powerful. Very powerful.

When she couldn't hang onto the ropes anymore, I carried her, with me still inside her, to the ground. She grabbed the throw and rolled over onto all fours, inviting me to take the most ancient of positions, which I happily did. At one point, I leaned up the length of her back, wrapped my arms around her, and milked her breasts as

I'd seen dairymen do cattle teats. She moaned and cried out, begging me to keep going, to never stop, to enjoy her, all of her. Every move, every part of every act, seemed the most natural thing in the world, as though I'd been with her all my life.

She led me back into the house eventually, stopping for a drink of water in the kitchen and to clean up our feet. Then we went back to the bed, where I dropped, exhausted. She begged me for one more time, with the promise that we'd sleep afterward.

"What do you want from me, woman?" I laughed, too tired to even try to imagine what she had in mind.

"A good old hard fuck," she responded, an edge in her voice. "Hard and fast. A little pain goes a long way. And you can twist, pull, or bite whatever you like."

I'd never, ever, had a woman talk to me like that, and it was a turn-on the likes of which I'd never enjoyed before. The manliest part of me rose to the occasion in a matter of seconds. She used some other language I'd been told ladies never used, and I loved it, asked her to beg me, talked back to her the same way. After I'd pulled her nipples out a good four inches, twisted them around so many times she'd practically screamed, and sucked and chewed most of the skin off of them, I tore into her like a man possessed, and she urged me on, crying out, "Harder, faster, deeper, baby. Don't you have more? Please, please, I want more!" I watched in amazement as she stimulated herself with one hand while I pounded her over and over, her other hand pulling my hair and twisting it around her fingers. I exploded deep inside her as she drove herself crazy, her head thrown back, pelvis thrusting wildly. Two more strokes, and she shuddered and went limp. It was over. There wasn't another drop in me.

I remember pulling her close again, lightly kissing her eyelids, her cheeks, her lips. If I'd held my hand a half inch above any area on her body, I'm sure a current would've passed between us that could power all of Ashville. Her hair was everywhere, as was mine, and she trembled slightly in my arms as I stroked the mass of blond waves. I looked down at the length of our bodies intertwined, appreciating the beauty of her white skin against my darkness. Several strands of our hair lay together on my chest, and I couldn't help but make a mental snapshot of the moment, the shiny blond and the glossy dark brown hair wrapped and twisted into one strand, our legs and bodies fused into a solid oneness. I twirled the hair together, as though that would keep us locked in each other's arms permanently. "You okay?" I whispered, stroking her cheek.

"Excellent," she whispered back, touching my lips with her fingertips. "I've never felt this close to anyone. I hope you realize I've fallen for you," she added, her voice a bit hesitant. "I've never felt that free with any man, even David. You have a marvelous effect on me."

"Well, I certainly hope you've fallen for me," I teased, touching her nipple lightly. "I'd hate to think I'd wasted that much bodily fluid on someone to whom I'm just a passing fancy. Besides, I'm a fabulous lover, and I'm completely irresistible!" She laughed and kissed me.

She knew what I meant. And so did I. As erotic as the night had been, there had been no hesitation, no embarrassment, not a single apology, and there had been nothing dirty or vulgar or obscene about it. It was incredible, but it was also more than wild animal sex, and we both knew it. I kissed her shoulder, then drew her arm out and kissed down the inside of its length. That's when I noticed it for the first time, her arm turned just the right direction in the candlelight.

On the inside of her left wrist was a tattoo of a tiny Celtic fan.

The barn was warm for a cold night. It was probably from the animals and their excrement, which generated copious amounts of heat, a thing to which any livestock farmer would attest. He shuffled toward the back of the barn behind her, past cows and a few chickens, to a plank door. When she swung it open and walked inside with the lantern, he drew in a sharp breath.

It held nothing but bales of hay, stacked high and wide, with a path down the middle. Claire proceeded down the path and when they came out the other side, the hay bales had been reduced to only one layer. Their surface was fairly large and even. Before Bill could ask why they were there, why she'd led him behind that door, Claire disappeared into a corner and came back with something beautiful and soft.

A quilt. If he remembered correctly, the pattern was called a Single Wedding Ring, and fairly rare at that. It was beautiful in its simplicity, put together with tiny patches of fabric in various colors and patterns, and to him it fairly glowed in the lantern light. He watched as Claire spread it over the bales of hay, and his heart raced around inside his chest like a mouse in a round room. When she'd gotten it exactly the way she wanted, she whispered, "I have to turn the lantern down now. Wouldn't want old Mr. Garrity to know we're out here." Once the lantern light had faded to just a flicker, Claire climbed onto the quilt and reached out to Bill.

Logic flew out the window; reason took a long walk. She was so lovely, her pale, china-like skin and those luminous eyes, and Bill wanted to lose himself in them for as long as he could. He dropped his crutches and climbed with awkward movements into the center with her. "Claire, I . . ."

She pressed a delicate finger to his lips. "I don't know what you're about to say, but don't, please don't," she whispered. "I want to be with you. I've been dreaming about it, what it would be like, and I want it. I want you." She leaned into him and kissed his lips lightly.

Bill couldn't think; he could only want deep down within his core. He needed this beautiful woman, but he didn't want to damage her, ruin her, spoil her beauty or trust. "Do you love me?" her eyes questioned more than her lips.

"I love you more than I thought it possible to love another human being. I'll love you until the end of time. And I'm so happy that you love me." He kissed her again, the scent of her powder filling his lungs and taking his breath away.

Claire took his hand and put it on top of hers, then began unbuttoning the front of her dress, a slow, excruciating task that had him throbbing inside his trousers. He finally came to his senses and took over the job for her. When the last button had been *undone, she pulled the dress away, then stood on her knees to pull her slip over her head.*

Nothing. Except for her panties, she was bare before him. Bill's eyes watered and his mouth went dry. Her breasts were perfect, never touched, rosy nipples hard and waiting for him. "I want to show you something," she whispered and turned out her left wrist. There, almost to the heel of her hand, was a small figure. "It's a tattoo," she smiled.

"A tattoo? Why on earth would you mark your body that way?" he cried out. "Does your father know?"

"No, and he never will. Look at it." In the dim light of the lantern, he couldn't tell what it was. Before he asked, she answered his unspoken question. "It's a Celtic fan. It reminds me of my Scottish-Irish love. Every time I see it, I think of you."

She'd marked herself to make her his, and Bill's heart almost leaped from his chest. He peeled off his shirt and, before he could get to them, Claire was unbuttoning and unzipping his trousers, her hand reaching into his fly, exploring, grazing his boxers in just the right place.

He shimmied out of the rest of his clothing except for the boxers, then drew her to him. When they fell on their sides onto the makeshift bed of their passion, Bill whispered, "This will be painful. That's not what I want, but that's how it will be. Are you sure you . . ."

"Positive." She grabbed his hand and placed his palm over her left breast. "I'm yours, Bill McInnes. Take me. Please take me," she begged as she rolled to her back, waiting, trembling.

He managed to slip his boxers off, and she gasped at the sight of his manhood, hard and ready for her. When her fingers brushed along its ridge lightly, he groaned and dove for her panties, slipping them off in an instant. Instead of trying to cover herself or looking embarrassed, she drew her feet back until her knees were bent and dropped her legs apart.

Open. Pulsing. Wet. Waiting for his grand entrance. Bill bent his head to her chest and took a rigid nipple into his soft lips, listening to her gasp first, then moan low and long. When he had positioned himself between her legs and knelt there, stroking himself, he retracted his foreskin and she looked at him with curiosity. "I don't understand. Why do you . . ."

"I'm not Jewish. We don't have a bris." She shot him an even more puzzled look. "I went to the library. I decided if I wanted to marry a Jewish girl, I should learn a little bit about Judaism."

Claire laughed. He loved that sound, the one telling him that whatever it was he'd said, it had made her happy. "Do you want to marry me, Bill McInnes?"

"Yes, Claire Steinmetz. I do. But it needs to be right. I've got to save up some money so we can have a place to live and all of that. We can't live in a cardboard box, you know!" His eyes were bright, even in the darkness, and Claire was even more certain that this was right, this coupling in this lowly place, straw in their hair and the smell of their sex everywhere.

"That's all I need to know. Make me yours, Bill. I want to belong to you." She licked her lips and smiled.

He and his heart needed no more encouragement. In one fluid motion, he pressed his maleness into her. It met with resistance, and he pushed heartily, feeling a giving away and a momentary rush of warmth — blood? — as he moved past the flesh barrier. At the snap, Claire cried out in pain, and bliss turned to alarm.

"Please, tell me you're all right," he groaned. "Oh, Claire, I need you so badly."

A single tear trickled down her cheek. "I'm fine. It hurt, but just for a second. Please, darling, please, this is what I want more than anything. Don't stop."

With that, Bill stroked his full length into her, feeling her tightness and willingness, and Claire cried out again, but not in pain. No, it was something else, a sense of accomplishment, a surrender. He'd never thought of her as wanton, but there it was — a woman wanting her man. As he began a rhythm he hoped would take her where he wanted to see her go, he bent again to her breast and sucked in a nipple, teasing it with his teeth and tongue. When he released it, he whispered to her, "Sweetheart, I don't expect anything to really come from this for you, but I would be thrilled if it gave you the pleasure of climax. Do you want that?"

Claire reached for his face and pulled it close to hers. "I'd love that, but all I really care about is having you inside me. We're one, Bill. We're together forever this way. Do you feel it?"

"I do." He wanted to repeat those two words, dressed in his Sunday best in front of a large group of people, as soon as he could. But for that one night, he'd just be a man in love with his woman, making love to her. More than once. So many times that he lost count. Watching her fly apart at his touch, cry out and beg for him as he pressed into her over and over, became his joy.

When he could turn her into Claire McInnes, his joy would be complete.

chapter 12

When I awoke Thursday morning, she was still in my arms, sleeping the slumber of the totally sexually satisfied. My self-esteem was at an all-time high. Here I was, almost fifty years old, and I'd met every need she'd had with high marks. I was pretty proud of myself, yes sir. "Studly" was back.

But I was sad too. For on this morning, a morning of celebration for two people who'd found what they didn't even realize they were looking for, the sun was shining. That meant that the rain was gone. And with no rain, the creek would soon drop back into its banks, and I'd have no excuse to stay. *Except for the incredible sex*, I chuckled to myself. And the fact that she had that tattoo. The problem was in finding a way to ask her about it. I'd rather have died than to tell her the real reason I'd come there in the first place. If she did know Roberts, did I really want to know now?

"Ms. Frazier, would you like some breakfast?" I asked as I poked her shoulder with my finger, trying to wake her up. She rubbed her eyes and squinted at me, her face falling when she noticed the sunshine streaming in the window. "Want some fresh fruit?" I added, hoping the thought would cheer her a little.

She kissed me and stammered, "What I really want is a shower." As she struggled to climb over me and get out of the bed, I slapped her on the behind playfully. She turned, smiled, and stumped off to the bathroom, robe in hand.

I lay there for a minute, thinking about the night before, the way she felt and looked. I wondered what I would do when my "moment of truth" came. The bridge wouldn't be washed out forever. Sooner or later, I'd have to make a decision. But I didn't want to think about that right now.

I stumbled down the hallway to the powder room, took a quick inventory of myself and my status, and made it to the coffeemaker to start a potful of liquid life. Just as I pressed the button, I heard something. It sounded like a voice. Someone singing. Was it Diana? No, it was a male voice. Where was that coming from? Just at that moment, someone pounded on the front door.

Even hearing the voice beforehand, the banging still scared the shit out of me, and I tiptoed to the porch, looking out the window to get a glimpse of the visitor. He was a delivery guy, complete with blue uniform and cap, carrying a package.

"How in the hell did you get back here?" I marveled.

"I found a tree I could shimmy across," he explained with a grin. The evidence was plain. Mud and water coated the inside of his pant legs, making him look as though he'd just ridden the dirtiest horse on the range bareback.

"You've got to be kidding." I shook my head in disbelief, signing for the package and taking it from his muddy hands. "Hey, but thanks. And please don't tell anyone you saw me here," I said with a grin, winking at him.

"You got it!" he laughed, and headed back up to the crest of the hill. I looked down at the package, wrapped in brown paper with a couple of labels on the front.

The address was to Diana N. Frazier at 19 Creekside Road. That didn't seem unusual. What was of interest was the return address label: New Century Publishing. I took a long look at the package. The size and shape were both right for . . . the label said "ARCs." Advanced reading copies – of what? I looked around the room. There wasn't another thing that hinted she would be receiving a package like this. As a matter of fact, I hadn't seen any papers of any kind anywhere in the house, no bills or clutter, no advertisements, nothing like that. Then I remembered the room at the end of the hall. If I recalled correctly, she'd left it unlocked when she came back to the living area the night before. I headed that way, package in hand.

The door opened silently, and my jaw dropped. Around the room, beautiful mahogany bookcases, similar to the ones near the fireplace, stood ceiling high, loaded with books and journals. A state-of-the-art laptop hummed on the huge desktop, sporting a screensaver of a forest scene with little animals scurrying about and a bear peeking out from behind a tree. There were books piled beside the laptop, books piled on an occasional table by a recliner on the other side of the room, books, books, and more books everywhere, as well as all kinds of papers, notes, and notebooks, plus an iPad. And three different kinds of printers, one with a built-in fax. Was this Nick Roberts' office? Did he work here? Or perhaps she typed for him. I looked at some of the volumes on the shelves, with titles like *Writing Down the Bones* and *Writing Life Stories*. There were other books too, by authors like Eudora Welty, Flannery O'Connor, and Bobbie Ann Mason, all primo southern writers. There were lots and lots of paperbacks. At the end of one shelf there were several odd-colored volumes and, checking the spines, I realized they were high school yearbooks. I chose the newest one and flipped through the senior pictures. It was a nice-sized school, and there were lots of seniors. I looked under Frazier, but didn't find her picture, of course; I'd assumed that was her family name, but maybe it was her late husband's name. I hadn't bothered to check but I knew if she were a senior in this particular volume, it would make her six years my junior. Flipping through the alphabet, I came to "r," wondering if Nick Roberts' picture would be there. Nope. I looked at the smiling faces, some with strange hairdos, and felt a little embarrassed for them. As I scanned the rows, I saw a familiar face. The hairstyle was different, but it was definitely Diana. The caption beneath the picture read "Salutatorian   Diana   Nicole . . ."   and   I   froze:

". . . Roberts." I felt weak, and my stomach churned with the realization of the truth.

I'd slept with Nick Roberts.

He paced, and with his every step she became more nervous. Finally, he said in a voice low and hoarse with anger, "Tell me, when did this take place?"

Claire's hands shook. "I don't know what you're talking about, Papa."

His fist slammed the tabletop. "You know exactly what I'm talking about! You gave away your purity to a crippled, Scotch-Irish, Catholic gentile! And you don't seem the least bit repentant about it! In fact, you're sitting here lying, telling me you don't know what I mean. Are you calling Mr. Garrity a liar?"

"No, I'm saying perhaps he didn't see what he thought he saw," Claire offered, her lower lip trembling.

"He saw exactly what he saw, more of my daughter's naked body than I'm comfortable with. And so did that gentile trash. That will end — this minute."

"Papa," she started gently, then let her tone go harsher, "Papa, you're talking about Bill just like other people talk about us. Don't you see? You're acting no better than those people who call us names because we're Jews."

"It's not the same, Claire. It's not the same at all." He continued to pace, and it made Claire more nervous than before.

"Well, I don't see how it's different, Arnold," a voice chimed in. Claire's mother had been listening and, surprisingly, came to her

aid. "You're treating that young man in ways you wouldn't want your daughters treated. That's what I see."

"And that young man treated my daughter like a whore!"

"He did not!" Claire screamed. "We're in love! He wasn't treating me like a whore! He was making love to me, and I wanted it! I wanted it!"

Before she could blink, her father's hand landed hard on her left cheek, and her head rocked. She cried out and her mother gasped. "If you're going to talk like a whore, I'm going to treat you like one!" her father yelled. "Go upstairs and bathe yourself! You stink like a whorehouse!"

Claire jumped up and ran up the stairs, her face stinging and her eyes burning. He couldn't treat her like that; she just wouldn't take it. She'd find a way to get away from him, from his control, from his domination. She loved Bill. She'd do what she had to do.

chapτer 13

The sound of the water coursing through the plumbing into the shower stopped, and I panicked. Shoving the yearbook back on the shelf, I grabbed the box and half ran, half slid out into the hall. I pulled the door closed behind me, and the latch clicked softly. I heard Diana call my name from the bathroom, as though she could hear the sound of the latch from behind the bathroom door. I ran back into the kitchen, poured myself a cup of coffee, placed the box on the table by the front door, and rushed back to the sofa, where I quickly settled in, trying to look as though I'd been there for a good while.

She appeared at the entrance to the hallway, wrapped in the pink flowered robe, a towel around her hair. "Were you in the bedroom just a minute ago?" she inquired, her brow pinched together in the center.

Damn, she'd heard the door. "No, beautiful, I wasn't. You probably heard the delivery man," I stated with false calmness, pointing to the package by the door.

"How the hell did he get here?" she asked, picking up the package and looking at the label. She put it down without commenting.

"You don't want to know. Just rest assured that no one else will try to do what he did," I said, sipping my coffee. As if on cue, the phone rang. It startled me so badly that I spilled coffee all over me. I yelped and she grabbed a towel, throwing it to me as she picked up the phone breathlessly.

"Hello?" she whispered into the phone, her voice a little shaky and cautious. "No, we're fine. Yes, Mr. Riley is here. He was trapped by the storm. We've got plenty of food. Uh-huh. I see. Well, thanks. Thanks very much." She hung up the phone.

"Who was that?" I questioned as she moved toward me and plopped down beside me on the sofa.

"That was the sheriff's office," she sighed. "They were checking on me. They also said your friends were worried about you. Maybe you should call them," she suggested, pointing to the phone.

My cell was long past dead, so that meant I had none of their cell numbers. I pulled down the phone book from the top of the refrigerator and looked up the Blue Bell Inn. I couldn't remember the room number, so I asked for Russ. It rang a couple of times, and Michael's voice answered.

"Michael!" I called out, sure he was still drunk. As usual, that was correct.

"Where the hell you been, man? We been worried sick 'bout ya," he mumbled, belching loudly.

"Where's Russ, Michael? Put him on the phone, okay? Get Russ, Michael." I heard him lay the phone on the nightstand and scream, "Russ! Phone!" There was a significant amount of noise and commotion, and I could hear Russ saying something about puking before he picked up the receiver.

"Steve! Where the hell are you?" he screamed into my ear. I held the phone out a bit until he'd stopped ranting, then answered him.

"I'm at a house at the end of Creekside Road. I'm okay, but the bridge across the creek has washed out, and I'm stuck here. My cell's dead and the phone's been out. They just fixed it. But I'm okay, really," I reiterated, hoping they wouldn't send out the National Guard for me. I was fine right where I was. Diana wandered past me and patted my butt on her way to the coffee pot. Yep, life was good and I was fine right where I was. I didn't need their help.

"Well, okay, pal, if you insist. When will you be back?" he asked insistently.

"What's wrong, Cherilyn worn out?" I chuckled. I saw Diana shoot me a look as if to say, *You're a fine one to talk*. I grinned at her and she winked back.

"No. Cherilyn's finer than fine." Was that a note of sarcasm I detected in his tone? "We were just worried about you, that's all. Keep in touch, okay?"

"Sure," I promised. "I'll do that." He hung up, and I put the receiver down, glad to be rid of him. The dream continued, and I really didn't want to wake up yet.

"What's that?" Diana asked, shushing me. I could hear it too. It was a car horn honking, and somebody yelling. She ran back to the bedroom and came back in the blink of an eye, trying desperately to pull on a pair of jeans under the shirt she'd thrown on. I'd put on mine earlier, and I headed for the front door. We ran up the driveway to the crest of the hill, and then down the other side toward the road, where an ancient, beat-up pickup truck sat in foot-deep water. The driver was honking his horn like crazy and yelling at the top of his lungs. Diana obviously recognized him and greeted him with "What are you doing out here, trying to get yourself killed?"

"I was worried 'bout you, Ms. Diana," the old man yelled, obviously concerned about her well-being. "Are you okay?"

"Yes, Clyde, I'm fine," she yelled toward him. "You can quit blowing the horn. I'm fine."

"Who's that guy wit ya?" he yelled again, pointing at me in a threatening manner.

"He was hiking and got trapped over here. But he's okay, really. I'm perfectly safe with him, Clyde. You go on back home. Thanks for checking on me, though. I appreciate it." She waved and turned to go. I stood still for a minute, and she growled under her breath, "Come on, Steve. If we don't head back to the house, he'll stand there and keep up a yelling conversation with us all day."

I took up for him. "Well, he had to yell," I said, trying to glean some sympathy for him. "He was too far away."

"He yells all the damn time. He's deaf as a stump," she snarled. I laughed. She had an admirer who was a lot older than me. That was cute and really sweet.

Strolling back to the house, I had a little time to process my discovery. She'd gotten the Nick part of the name from Nicole, and her family name was Roberts. But why had she kept the whole thing such a big secret? That explained the nice furnishings, the expensive computer, and the pricey clothes I'd spied in the back of her closet during a snooping foray. But why all the mystery?

She walked along on my right. I reached out for her left hand and pulled it up to my lips, kissing her knuckles, the underside of her wrist turned toward me as her arm bent upward. "Nice tattoo," I commented, looking for a reaction.

"Think so?" she asked, as if looking for my approval.

"Oh, yeah. It's a beaut. So delicate and sexy. A reminder of your heritage?" I asked, trying to get her to divulge her secret. She didn't waver.

"I guess so. I've got a collection of Celtic stamps, and I liked the design on one of them, so I asked a tattoo artist in Asheville to do it. Cost me three hundred bucks, but he did a good job." She admired it too, as though seeing it for the first time. When we reached the house, she climbed the steps and stopped on the second one, turning to me, hands on my shoulders, and kissed the top of my head. I put my arms around her waist and buried my face in the valley between her breasts, my mind racing. Her finger under my chin lifted my face up to hers. "I just can't believe how beautiful you really are," she whispered, and she kissed the end of my nose.

"And I can't believe how magical you are. You're like a fairy princess," I said as I stroked her hair. Turning to go in the door, she took my hand and drew me back into the living area, where we fell onto the sofa and lay side by side, me on my side against the back, her flat on the seat, looking up into my face. I could tell what was coming. The previous night had been too precious and intense to think this conversation wasn't going to happen. Might as well get it over with.

"I know what you're thinking," I offered without being asked.

"Oh, yeah? And just what am I thinking?" she teased, poking my arm with her finger.

"You're thinking about the bridge being fixed and wondering what's going to happen then," I stated plainly. She nodded. "Well, what do you think I should do, Diana? Help me out here."

She frowned. "I can't tell you what to do," she said gently after a second or two. "What do you want to do?"

"I want to take you back down the hall and bang the daylights out of you again, but that's beside the point," I laughed. She wasn't laughing.

"I'm being serious, Steve," she said, her voice firm and tense. "I can't tell you what to do."

"What do you want me to do?" I asked her, almost repeating myself. I could tell she was growing frustrated with the conversation, and her eyes flashed under her squinted, wrinkled brow line.

"What do you imagine I'd want you to do? Sleep with me and walk away? Don't you think that question is just a little bit ridiculous?" *Uh-oh,* I thought. *Our first fight.*

"I don't want to do that. I'd stay here forever if I could, you know that. But I have to make a living, and I can't do it here. Besides, we really don't know each other that well, in the traditional sense anyway," I reminded her. "Maybe I could come on weekends and spend time with you. We could have a regular kind of relationship, the kind other people have, get to know each other when we're no longer incarcerated." I grinned, thinking I was clever. She still wasn't laughing, but she didn't seem angry either. Instead, she was listening to me, trying to rationalize what I was saying, weighing it against what she really wanted.

"What would it take for you to stay here? I mean, what do you need that you couldn't have here?" she asked in all sincerity.

"Well, a steady income would be the number one requirement. I can't make a living freelancing. And you can't support me." That seemed like good bait. I waited, thinking at any moment she'd admit to me her authorship of the book, tell me about the money she had. She didn't.

"That's true. I'm not made of money. The insurance settlement won't last forever either," she said, resignation in her voice. Now it was my turn to get frustrated. I couldn't believe she'd just let me walk away, all because she wanted to keep her work a secret. Why was that so important? "Maybe your idea is best. Maybe we should see each other on the weekends. I could come there too sometimes, even in the middle of the week. But I never want to live somewhere else."

I didn't want to either. I thought about the last three days, the little house, the swing in the back, the pale lavender room, the smell of the gardenia shampoo, and the mountains, those beautiful mountains, surrounding the little cabin. More than anywhere else in the world, I was truly comfortable there, in that house, with that incredible woman. My desire to be with her had only grown from knowing she was capable of writing something so moving and powerful that it changed people's lives. I thought about Bill and Claire, about how Claire had died in the end. I didn't want that kind of ending for us or our relationship. Us. I hadn't even thought that word before. It sounded scary and exhilarating, horrific and magical, terrifying and electrifying all at the same time.

"We'll work something out, I promise. But for right now, let's just enjoy the time we have," I pleaded, stroking her hair. She stood and walked back down the hallway to the bedroom, and I followed a few steps behind. We stood beside the bed, and I drew the tee-shirt over her head, exposing her breasts, nipples already erect. She pulled my shirt up and over my head and, once it was off, I wrapped my tongue around a nipple and pushed her down onto the bed. The three of us made love: Diana, Nick Roberts, and me.

And two of us cried.

"I'm sure you've never seen this much money." It was meant as a slap in the face, but he was right – Bill had never seen that much money.

"But sir, I don't want your money. I love Claire. You can't pay me to stay away from her. I plan to marry her."

Mr. Steinmetz sat down and sighed. "That's not going to happen. You're not marrying my daughter. I've forbidden it, and I won't change my mind. That's that." He mopped his forehead with a plain white handkerchief. "This money will allow you to go to school, get some kind of education so you won't always be an ignorant gentile. Or it will let you find another woman, one of your own kind, and buy yourself a place to live and fornicate."

No one had ever talked to Bill that way. This man might be Claire's father, but Bill had had just about enough of his hate. He chose his words carefully. "Mr. Steinmetz, Claire and I have not fornicated. We . . ."

"Yes you have! Don't try to deny it! Mr. Garrity saw you. He saw you deflowering my virgin daughter on a bale of hay. Does she really mean so little to you that you'd take her innocence in a nasty place like a barn?"

"We were together in the barn because we can't be together anywhere else and in any other way. And that's because of you." There. He'd said it. It felt good to fire back at the angry man, a man he'd never done anything to except to love that man's daughter. He thought all fathers wanted their daughters to find a man who loved them. Apparently that meant nothing to this man.

Mr. Steinmetz turned his back to Bill. "You are not going to marry my daughter. Take this money. Use it to make your sorry life better."

At that moment, it all made sense to Bill. He should take the money. Then he could buy a place for them to live, something nice, and they could get married and live there. And it would be poetic justice, doing so at her father's expense. Bill fought a grin.

"Okay, sir. I guess there's no use in trying to fight you. Give me the money and I'll go away." He held out his hand.

Mr. Steinmetz reached out and slapped the paper money into Bill's waiting palm. As he did, Bill snapped his fingers shut over Mr. Steinmetz's hand and growled, "But one of these days you're going to regret this."

chapter 14

We spent most of the rest of Thursday in bed, coming out only for the most meager of sustenance. We drank lots of coffee too. I wanted to go outside in the sunshine and do the wild thing, but she was afraid she'd get a sunburn. When I suggested the shade of the maple tree out back, she was the first one out the door, packing a quilt. She lay back in the spotted sunshine that made it through the leaves of the tree, her knees pulled up and to either side of her chest, and me on my knees, hands resting on her shins, looking down at her, moving in and out of her, watching it all. The power I felt was overwhelming, electric. She brought her hands down to her sides and under her, reaching around, stroking the insides of my thighs and anything else she could reach, keeping me bigger and harder than I'd ever been. I felt as though I'd burst. When I did let go, she knew, could feel the surge, the warmth and wetness. I pumped gallons into her, and she took them all, ready for more in mere minutes.

The night was no different. We drifted in and out of sleep, vacillating between making love and just plain banging each other during waking periods. At some point she was astride me, riding me for all she was worth, and I remember telling her, "I think you're trying to kill me! Is this what happens when you save up for six years?"

She laughed, quick to remind me, "You were the one who said we should make the most of the time we had!" I slid my hands up her tummy and held them there, feeling me inside her again, then I moved them farther up and held her breasts tightly while she moved on top of me. The ending was slow and sweet, and I went limp inside her as she lay on my chest, arms around my neck, hair across my face, our bodies tired and sore. We were like two fifteen-year-olds, exploring each other's bodies, acting as if we alone had discovered the oldest pleasure known to man, were the only ones to realize that penises and vaginas fit together. There was a wonderment, a sparkle to it all, and even after all the women I'd been with, I felt as though Diana had stolen my virginity, as though she was the very first woman with whom I'd ever become one. I remembered Bill and Claire and the nights they'd spent in each other's arms in the creaky old barn, straw in their hair and their time together dwindling, just like ours.

When my eyes opened Friday morning, I could hear some kind of heavy equipment. I tried to wake Diana, sleeping soundly on my arm, and rolled her over enough to pull myself free. She stirred and asked me what was going on.

"I hear a bulldozer or something," I reported, pulling on my jeans to make the trip down the drive to the road. "Come with me," I pleaded, not wanting her out of my sight for a single minute. I felt sure the time we'd spent alone in our sheltered environment was rapidly coming to an end.

"No way," she whined, burying her face in the pillow. "I don't know if I can walk or not. I'm pretty sore. And my nipples hurt. I think they're broken." I rolled her over and looked at them. They were swollen and red, but they weren't "broken," whatever that was supposed to mean.

"Guess you need to wean your baby!" I laughed, slapping her on the thigh. She snorted and rolled back over.

The sky was blue and clear, decorated with little white, puffy clouds, when I looked out the front window. I looked toward the road, and I could see something that looked like diesel exhaust wafting above the ridge. I slipped my boots on and headed toward the road.

My trip over the ridge brought an eyeful. There, at the end of the drive, was an enormous truck with an army emblem on the side. With it was a small crane, big enough to take care of the job underway. They had hoisted up a transportable steel bridge with the crane, and were in the process of unfolding it and placing it across the creek. The roadbed itself was completely dry, or at least no longer underwater, and there were several official-looking guys wandering around. One noticed me and waved.

"Hello!" he shouted. "I'm Major Wallace from the Army Reserves. We're down here doing some flood relief, you know, public service stuff and all that. Anyway, we should have your bridge in place in a few hours. You folks okay over there?"

"Thanks. We're fine. Appreciate what you're doing. What's all this going to cost?" I questioned, wondering what Diana was going to say about it.

"Nothing, sir. It's something we do for private citizens and communities when there's been a natural disaster. You got enough food over there?" he asked, having a hard time believing we were surviving the ordeal without their help.

"Yes sir, we've got everything we need." If he only knew what I had in that house, the amazing thing we had together, he wouldn't ask that. "Thanks again." I waved and turned to go back up the hill.

When I reached the house, Diana was in the kitchen, making coffee. She was moving kind of slowly, and I walked up behind her, wrapping my arms around her waist. She reached back and ran her hand down the side of my face. I kissed her palm and turned her around to face me. She stood on her tiptoes to kiss me, and I felt the urge to weep. I wanted to hold her like this forever, her breasts pressed against my chest, the countertop pressing into the small of my back as she leaned her body weight against me. She pulled back and sighed deeply, her hands locked behind my neck, looking up into my face. Her eyes looked moist, and I could tell she was fighting back tears. "What are we going to do, Steve? Please tell me. What's going to happen to us?" A tiny tear rolled down her cheek, and I brushed it away with my thumb. But it was too late. I felt white-hot, stinging wetness on my own face, and I couldn't hold it in anymore. I'd never cried in front of a woman, unless you counted when my mother died, and then it was just during the funeral. She stroked my hair, her fingers working from my temples back and down the length, drawing the ends over my shoulders, working the strands through her shaking fingers as I fought to choke back the tears now coursing down my cheeks. In my mind I saw my office, my chair, the desk and credenza both covered with work, the phone ringing, people stopping in the doorway to chat. What would I say to them? How could I go back there, sit in that office, pretend that nothing had happened? I felt her body stiffen, and I clutched her shoulders, pushing her back to look directly into her face.

"This isn't over," I said, unsure whether I was trying to convince her or myself. "It's not over, you hear me? I won't let this die, won't let it go. I'm not sure what we'll do, but we'll do something, even if it's wrong." She nodded, her chin quivering.

"I believe you, Steve." There was resolution in her voice. "I trust you." That was all I needed to hear. I took her by the hand and marched her down the hallway to the bedroom. Once in the room, I sat her down on the side of the bed and prowled through the nightstand until I found pen and paper.

"Okay, here," I said, scribbling furiously. "Here's my phone number at home, and my phone number at work." I continued scratching on the paper. "This is my cell number. Here's my pager number. They're on all the time, so you can reach me anywhere at any time. Here's my address," I added as I scribbled more, "and this is my Social Security number. My friend Russ? Here's his phone number." I pulled out my wallet and checked the various compartments until I found a little piece of paper I keep hidden in it. "This is my attorney's phone number," I told her, an alarmed look spreading across her face, "and here's the number of my regular physician. And my e-mail address. And this is the website address for the paper, and it has a link to me on one of the pages. And this is my driver's license number," I went on, "and my license plate number too. I have a dark blue Mercedes, an eighty-nine model two-door coupe." The writing helped me focus, cut the pain, gave me something to do. She sniffled as she watched. "Don't lose this, you hear me?" I could hear the desperation in my own voice, hear it breaking as I shoved the paper into her hand, feeling like I'd done all I could do, still frightened and unsteady. "Don't cry on it. You'll smudge the ink," I barked, and her shoulders began to heave as great wracking sobs poured out of her soul, washing over me like molten lava, burning my ears. As I sat down beside her she fell over, her head in my lap, and continued to sob, quietly then, a pitiful, resigned quality in her petitions. My hands covered my face and I waited, wanting to comfort her, wanting her to comfort me, not knowing what else to do. We crawled onto the bed together, eyes swollen and red, noses running, clinging to each other through the end of the world, our world.

We napped, and I dreamed. In my dream, the house was the same, but bigger. One door led to the dining room which appeared to be my office. That allowed me to be there all the time. I worked at the dining room table, and Christopher, one of the guys from graphics, dropped by the dining room door and chatted for awhile. The phone rang, and it was my mom, inviting us to dinner, which I excitedly agreed to after we had established that she wasn't really dead. I took my briefcase into my office, and in it was an enormous box of condoms. Diana came into my office, and we made love on the table. Christopher, the same guy from graphics, walked by and said we looked great together, and he took our picture, up on the table, going at it like two bunnies on a sunny spring day. It was a great dream.

We both roused about the same time, right around noon. She shuffled down the hall to fix some kind of meal, and I stayed on the bed, thinking about all that had taken place in that room. I knew she'd never see it the same way again. I didn't want to leave there, not that way. My wallet was lying on the nightstand, and I picked it up to shove it in my back pocket. I'd placed her wedding band on the nightstand, and I knocked it off as I moved my wallet. Picking it up, I opened the nightstand drawer to drop it in.

There was a familiar looking piece of paper in it. The logo was the familiar part: New Century Publishing. But it was no regular piece of paper. It was a check, a check for eight thousand dollars. I could see another one too; it was for fourteen thousand seven hundred dollars. There were several more, about eight or nine, totaling nearly one hundred thousand dollars as best I could tell. I wanted to say something, but I just couldn't. My mind was made up. I never wanted her to know that I knew about Nick Roberts, about the book, about any of those things. She couldn't know. She had to believe that my entrance into her life had been an accident, a coincidence. I pushed the drawer shut and tried not to think about it. She called my name, and I made it to the kitchen in time to see a uniform coming to the door. Without waiting for him to knock, I walked straight out onto the porch and met him.

"Hi again, Major Wallace," I smiled, hoping he didn't notice how red my eyes were. "How's it going?"

"We're all finished," he reported in an efficient manner. "The bridge is in place, and we've tried it with a couple of our vehicles. You're all set. Is there anything else we can do for you?"

Yeah, you bastard, I wanted to scream, *you can rip the damn thing up and take it back with you. We didn't ask for it, and we don't want it.* Instead, I smiled. "Nope. Thanks. Thanks very much. Thank the army for us too, would you?" He shook my hand and marched back over the hill. By that time Diana had come to the doorway, watching and listening. I turned and saw her standing there, still and quiet. "Let's have some lunch," I suggested, trying to force a smile.

We ate in virtual silence, an occasional comment on the tuna or the bread. I wanted to talk about our future, about all the things we'd do together, but it seemed kind of pointless. My mind was already in high gear, mentally trying to remember all the engagements I had over the months to follow, wondering how to make time to come back to the little house and do the things that had to be done. But I would. I knew I would.

She stayed in the kitchen to clean up while I moped back down the hallway to the bedroom, headed for the shower. I passed the room with the locked door, and wondered if it had been locked back, but I didn't try the knob. The water was warm and refreshing, but it washed away only part of the tension. I'd been standing in the steady flow for about five minutes, motionless, when the tub door opened and she stepped in. She kissed me, a sweet little peck right on the lips, and reached for the soap. We showered, no funny business, just two people getting clean together, making peace with what would happen. When we were finished, I used one of those big fluffy towels again and wondered when I'd see another one that huge and soft. She was right behind me, and we dressed in silence, neither one wanting to break the spell. I didn't want to be the one responsible for saying the words, acknowledging what was about to happen, as if ignoring it would keep it from taking place.

I headed into the living area and looked around. My backpack was on the back porch, and I searched around, making sure I hadn't left anything lying about. Her eyes were watching me, I knew, but I couldn't turn around to meet her gaze. Once the bag was packed, I walked toward the door.

"Walk with me to the ridge?" I asked, holding out my hand, reaching for hers. She grabbed it and clung to my arm, walking beside me until we reached the ridge. We stopped, and I turned to face her.

"Here," she said, stuffing something into my backpack. "Those are my numbers and addresses and such. You might forget how to find me." I knew that would never happen.

"Thanks. I promise I won't lose them." Fishing for something positive to say, I quickly added, "And as soon as I get back home, I'll check my calendar and let you know when I can come here, okay?"

"I'll expect that," she grinned, reaching up to touch my face. I hoped I'd remember that feeling, that touch, that it would be enough to hold me until I could get back there.

The driveway seemed shorter than before, hopelessly shorter, the road much too close. I made it halfway down before I turned to look back, to see her brave face, a single tear dripping from her jawline. It couldn't be put off any longer.

Marching back up the hill and right up to her, I took both her hands in mine and looked straight into her eyes, those calm, gunmetal blue eyes I'd been drawn into the first time I'd seen them. And I said it, meant it, more so than any other time in my life.

"I love you, Diana. Don't doubt that, ever."

Her lower lip quivered uncontrollably, and she mouthed the words back, but no sound came out. I kissed her, tasting her salty tears, or perhaps my own, then turned and strode down the hill without looking back. By the time my feet hit the road, I was weeping like I'd never wept before, my vision blurred, my eyes unable to focus. I couldn't look back, because I knew what I'd see, but I couldn't help myself. I turned, peering back over my left shoulder.

The hill was bare. She was gone.

Bill waited all afternoon for Claire to come into town. She always came in on Fridays before the Sabbath started. When she never appeared, he wondered if something was wrong, if she was ill. He had no way of seeing her unless she left the house, so he walked toward the big brick Georgian and waited.

When he saw her come out, he tried to think of a way to talk to her. He watched as the family got into their car and headed toward the synagogue, and he tried to come up with a way to get a message to her. Once they were gone, he pulled out a scrap of paper and a stub of a pencil and wrote her a note. Her bedroom window was on the ground floor, so he opened it just a crack, placed the paper on the window sill, and closed it back. He could only wait.

In the darkness of the barn, Bill watched for Claire's pale form to come down the long path from their house and through the dense tree line. After a while, he curled up on a bale of hay, the same one on which they'd made love, and fell asleep. When he woke in the morning, he made his way back to the boarding house where he stayed and wondered what to do next.

Claire found the scrap of paper Bill had left, and wondered why he'd bothered. Her father had given him what he'd really wanted; he'd recounted to her how eager Bill had been to take the money, how he said he'd finally gotten what he was looking for after all, and had vowed to never see Claire again. The note simply asked her to come to the barn, and she knew what that meant. He wanted to have relations with her again. Apparently that was the other thing he'd wanted from the beginning, but she'd have none of that. Her love had been sold, and all she had was bitterness. She pulled up her sleeve, looked down at the beautiful little tattoo, and wept.

chapter 15

By the time I reached the connecting road behind the convenience store, I'd splashed some water from the creek on my face and pulled myself together. I turned, then turned again, and walked back up the main street toward the motel, scuffing my feet and kicking at rocks as I went. Nothing looked the same. The store, the little bank building, everything looked different, sad somehow. When I reached the motel, the back tailgate of the SUV was open, and Russ and Michael were throwing their bags in. Russ spotted me first, and he stood in the dust in front of the little motel, hands on hips.

"Well, look what the cat dragged in," he shrilled, grinning from ear to ear. "Trapped, huh? I bet you were. Get some?"

"Shut up, Russ. What's going on here?" I asked, looking in the back of the SUV.

"We're leaving, that's what. We'd decided if you didn't show up today, we were going to leave your ass," mumbled Michael, throwing something else. "This trip's been one big bust. We didn't find Nick Roberts, we didn't find a bar, we didn't find a damn thing." Little did they know.

"Where's Jim?" I quizzed, his absence obvious.

"He's with Cherilyn," Russ said, an air of contempt about him.

"Huh?" I knew I'd been gone, but this was a little confusing.

"Yeah," Russ continued. "Seems he mentioned possibly purchasing some land for a funeral home here. She went hog-wild looking for property for him to view and, well, one thing led to another." He looked a little bewildered. "I swear, I must be losing it. I've never been thrown over for Jim before. If you'd told me this would happen," he babbled, "I'd have told you that you were insane. But sure enough . . ."

I stopped him. "You mean Jim's with Cherilyn?" Maybe I'd been gone longer than I thought.

"That's what the man said," Michael interrupted. "Now, you going back or not? If you are, load your stuff up. If you're not, this bus is pulling out without you, so step aside." He threw open the front passenger door and climbed in.

I rushed in and started grabbing stuff, tossing it into my suitcase. There was a phone book for the area on top of the little bedside table, and I deposited it in my suitcase too. It might come in handy for ordering flowers or something. Only a few minutes passed while I worked to load things up, and we were on the road. Jim, they'd told me, had decided to fly back the next week. This would probably go down in the history books as one of his best trips.

The journey back was agony. I rode in silence, replaying the scenes of the last few days in my head. Diana smiled in most of them, and I could feel her touch, see the dappling of the sun through the leaves on her milky skin as she lay on the quilt in the back yard. My backpack was wedged firmly between my feet as I sat in the back seat, and I remembered the piece of paper she'd pushed into my backpack. I fished it out and found it carried pretty much the same information on her that I'd given her on me. I folded it carefully and tried to put it in my wallet, but it was too hard to do strapped into the back seat. There was a pocket on the outside of my backpack, and I placed the paper, almost reverently, in the pocket, zipping it shut for safekeeping, making a mental note of its whereabouts. That was when I noticed something odd in my backpack, something with corners, something hard. I opened the pack and plunged my hand down in it, feeling around. When I'd finally located the object, I pulled it out and stared at it in amazement. My heart melted.

It was the Steinbeck novel, where it all began. I'd never owned anything more priceless than that little volume. Stashed back in the backpack, it was safe and headed home with me.

Bill had disappeared. Claire had tried to find him, to talk to him, but he was nowhere to be found.

She'd overheard her father downstairs, talking to her mother, laughing about how he'd finally talked Bill into taking the money, making it clear that he'd never be allowed to marry Claire. He laughed about how broken Bill had looked. Why had Bill done that, taken the money? She wanted to know, and she wanted to hear it from him.

The barn called to her, and she made her way out into the night, quilts over her shoulder, intending to sleep where they'd spent that glorious night together. She spread out the quilt on the bales of hay, then crawled under the second one. As she lay there, her heart aching, she turned onto her side and there she saw it: A note, stuck on a nail, right there. She read it and her heart broke again as she understood why her assumption about Bill's disappearance had been wrong. The only man to behave dishonorably in the whole mixed-up, muddled, hurtful mess was her father.

And Claire snapped. In the middle of the night she packed her bags and left. Taking the only highway out of town, she stopped along the way and bought a few slices of bread, then begged a glass of water from the store owner. When she found her way to the city, she stood on the sidewalk with a sign made from a grocery sack until she'd managed to sell the car. The money from it wasn't much, but it was something.

Two weeks later, she was exhausted. The factory paid enough for her to have a decent room at a boarding house and two meals a day, but the work was wearying and repetitive. She looked forward to leaving in the evenings, even though it meant she'd go to her room alone and spend the night crying.

Sometimes she walked to the private detective's office. Her brown saddle oxfords were beginning to show the wear and tear of walking the city streets just as her hands and back were succumbing to the pain of standing all day, folding and pressing shirts, her arms scalded from the steam. Her shoes squeaking and feet aching, she climbed the stairs to the third floor office where he sat, taking her money and giving her nothing in return. No, he hadn't found Bill. Yes, he was looking. No, he had no news for her, and he'd let her know when he did.

And so she'd leave the private detective's office, climb back down the stairs, and walk the eight blocks back to the boarding house. After a while, her saddle oxfords didn't squeak anymore. They were worn and almost past their time. Some days it seemed they took on a life of their own. They took her to work and back, and sometimes back to that dreary little office, almost like they had their own thoughts. There were days she'd arrive at the boarding house after work and not even remember the trip. On those days, she was glad those shoes had a memory, even if it were of better times. No amount of shoe polish helped them, and after two months, they started to crack and split.

After three months, the soles gave way. She tried to tie them together, but it was useless. New ones were too expensive on her salary, so eventually she went to a used clothing store and bought a pair only a little better than the old ones.

But she couldn't throw those saddle oxfords away. They knew the way home. And they knew the way to the barn. Every night she dreamed of being back in that barn in the arms of the man who loved her. She'd sleep in those shoes, praying that they'd take her back there.

And every morning, she awoke alone, staring at that tattoo.

chapter 16

I tried to relax on Saturday and catch up on some work, but I had trouble concentrating. The silence inside the walls of the house that no longer felt like home was deafening. Holding off as long as I could, busying myself with laundry and mowing the grass, I waited until about six that evening and realized I couldn't stand it any longer.

The phone rang twice on the other end, and she picked it up.

"Hello?" I was pretty sure I heard angels singing.

"Hey, gorgeous! I'm doing laundry. What are you doing?" I pictured her face, smiling that perfect smile, her eyes almost squinted shut.

"Just having a bite to eat. And thinking about this beautiful, sexy guy I met the other day. You should meet him." She laughed. Her laughter sounded like wind chimes on a warm day in May, and the ice water in my veins began to warm.

We didn't really have anything to talk about, but we just couldn't hang up the phone. I just wanted to hear her say something, anything, that would draw me back to the house, to the bed, or the sofa, or the bar stool at the counter.

"Still sore?" I teased her.

"Reveling in it," she assured me, her voice soft and serious. "If the pain will help me remember, I'll gladly hurt forever." My chest tightened, and I felt my eyes filling up again, ready to spill over. "Rested up yet?"

"No." And that was the truth. I'd tossed and turned the night before, unable to even close my eyes. I needed the sound of the rain on the tin roof, that constant roar, to drown out the sounds of my own breathing. "I don't sleep well away from home." She made a sound, a tiny one, and I realized that she was crying softly like I'd cried in the night. The air in the room seemed stagnant, and I fought to breathe. "I guess I'd better go." Then I remembered something important. "Hey, guess what?" I asked, trying to sound bright and cheerful.

"Can't imagine," she answered, fighting for composure.

"I checked my calendar. I can come down next weekend on Friday night and stay until Sunday night."

"Really?" she squealed. "Great. We can cook out. I bought a new grill when I went to Asheville this morning. You can take its propane virginity."

"You went to Asheville this morning?" I was more than a little shocked.

"Yes," she repeated herself calmly. "I went to Asheville this morning." She paused. "I had to get out of the house. I couldn't stand it anymore." If anyone could understand that, I could.

"Well, get ready, 'cause I'll be there Friday evening. Diana?" I stopped, the question in my voice a way to make sure she was listening.

"What, Steve?"

"I love you, baby."

"Oh, god, I love you too. And I miss you. It's awful." Her voice was breaking again.

"We'd better go, don't you think? We could do this all evening, but it wouldn't help," I said, trying to make things better.

"I know." Then she asked, "Can you send me a picture? I don't even have a picture of you." I heard it again, the cracking in her voice, as she added, "I don't want to forget what you look like."

"No, I won't send it. I'll bring it when I come next weekend, and I want one of you too. Maybe we can drive into Asheville, go to dinner and take in a movie or something. I bet we could find someone who'd take a picture of us together. That's what I'd really like," I said, thinking how it would look on my desk or, better yet, on my bedside table.

"I can't wait. I'll see you then. Please don't forget," she tagged on the end.

"Forget what?" I asked.

"Me."

I feigned indignation. "Never. I'll talk to you sometime this week, okay?"

"Sure," she said, fake hopefulness leeching out of her voice.

I hung up the phone and wondered what was going on there in Ebbs Mill. Were the coyotes howling yet, or had they waited? What about that cat I'd seen? Was it hanging around the back door? Everything going on in my world seemed so unimportant and small. I wondered if things would ever be good or right again.

I played golf with Russ most of the day on Sunday. We only saw each other a few times during the year other than the trip, and this year we'd barely seen each other even then. We'd always had the kind of friendship that was current regardless how long it had been since we'd spoken. One call, and it was like we'd spoken just yesterday. I have to hand it to him, he managed to hold back until the fifth hole, and then he couldn't wait anymore. We stood in the shade of the tree line just off the tee.

"Okay, spill it," he blurted out, startling me. "I can't stand it. What happened up there? Something's different. I can't figure out what it is, but you don't even look the same. Just exactly what went on up there?"

I'd always been open and honest with Russ. He'd heard intimate details of my sex life, mostly in the form of bragging over conquests, for years. But I didn't want to share any of my feelings, or especially activities, with Diana. It was all too fresh, too painful. He hammered away.

"Come on, Steve. Talk to me. I could describe the genitals of most of your girlfriends better than their gynecologists could," he snapped. "What's going on with you here? You're acting really strange. Talk to ol' Russ. Tell me all about it."

"Well, ol' Russ," I began, mocking him, "it's kind of personal."

"Whoaaaaaa! Too personal for Russ?" He looked like he'd just been hit with a couple of defibrillator paddles. "How can that be? Was she that good, or that bad?"

"Shut up, Russ. I don't want to talk about it." I chose another club and swung it back and forth lightly. I knew he wouldn't stop until he'd gotten the information he wanted, in detail. I could feel my nerves start to jangle.

"She nailed you, didn't she, buddy?" He taunted me, his lip curled in a mocking smile. "A woman finally got to the big guy. She must be some lay."

"I said shut up, Russ. I mean it. Just stop." My cheeks started to burn, and I felt hot and flushed, like a fuse had been lit.

"Come on, Steve. Tell me about it. What happened? How many times did you do her? Did she give you a hummer? Nice and tight? Come on, talk to . . ."

I don't remember a lot of what happened next, but another golfer a hole away said I grabbed Russ by the collar and smacked him up against a tree. I must have bounced him good, because it knocked him out. The next thing I knew, a couple of other people were pulling me off of him, and I was still trying to get at him.

When he came to, I was feeling pretty bad about what had happened, and I told him so. He looked up at me and said something so profound, so un-Russ-like, I knew it either had to be true or I'd inflicted a closed-head injury.

"You're head-over-heels in love with this one, aren't you?" I just nodded. "Damn! You're nearly fifty years old! What in the hell took you so long!" He slapped me on the shoulder and shook my hand. He didn't remember the being knocked out part too well, and I was glad for that. A friendship saved by unconsciousness.

I sat down in my recliner later that evening, holding *The Celtic Fan* in my hands. The picture on the front haunted me. I could almost feel the tender surface of her arm, and I traced the tiny picture with my finger. That's when I remembered the backpack.

Holding it between my legs, I began to pull out items one by one. A smashed, melted granola bar went in the trash, but I could put the unopened bottles of water in the refrigerator. The Steinbeck hardcover was placed carefully on top of *The Celtic Fan*, like a miniature shrine being built right there on the table. I tugged at something else that turned out to be a shirt, one Diana had worn a few days before. I tried to remember. It was the one I'd taken off of her the first night we'd spent together. I held it to my face. Soft and sweet, it smelled of lavender, faintly, but still there. My eyes closed, and I pressed it to my cheek, enjoying its softness, remembering the way she looked in the candlelight when I'd stripped it from her. Within minutes I had a problem I wished she could be present to fix, and I stroked myself, aching for her hands, wanting her more than I'd ever wanted any woman. But I'd see her on the weekend, I promised myself. If she'd waited six years, I could wait until then. It was just five days, but a very long five days.

Work. Eat. Sleep. Repeat.

Bill did nothing else. His only consolation was the money Mr. Steinmetz had thrust on him, sitting in a bank account, drawing interest. He contributed to it every payday too. He had more than enough to buy a nice little house, but he kept living in the boarding house, saving his money.

And he thought of Claire every waking moment and in his sleep. He wondered what she was doing. Was she happy? Had she found someone new? Probably. She was a beautiful girl and she'd have no shortage of young Jewish men courting her.

He'd been in the city for three months when a familiar face caught his eye. In a group of girls, paper sacks in their hands, he spotted Claire's younger sister. He remembered her from the night she'd answered the door. Work didn't matter; he forgot he was supposed to be there and spent the morning following the group from a distance. They were apparently on some kind of trip from school.

When they finally stopped for lunch, Bill bought a sack lunch from the grocery on the corner across from the park, then crossed the street to where the children were. He sat down on a bench near the little cluster of adolescents and waited. It didn't take long and he felt a presence, someone looking at him.

He looked up into Claire's sister's face. "Hi!" he chirped.

"Hello," she smiled. "I remember you. You're the man my father hates."

Bill's face fell. "I know. But you need to know that I didn't do anything to make him hate me. Really."

A sad smile spread across her face. "I know. He hates a lot of people. That's how he is. But I don't. And Claire doesn't. And my mother doesn't. She tried to get him to let Claire see you, but he got really angry."

Bill didn't need to know any of that. It didn't matter. What did matter was Claire. "So how is your sister these days?"

She shook her head. "I don't know."

Bill's heart froze. "What do you mean, you don't know?"

"She's gone." The girl looked stricken. "She disappeared. I think she ran away. One morning we got up and her things were gone. The car was gone. My father found it, but some strange man was driving it, said he bought it from a friend of his. My father never found the friend. We don't know what happened to Claire." She stopped and a tear trickled down her cheek. "I hope she's okay."

Bill swallowed hard. "I hope so too. If you hear from her," he said, trying not to choke, "will you please tell her that I still love her and I'd like to talk to her?"

She nodded. "I will. She was happiest when she was with you."

"Lila? Lila, who are you talking to? Come on, we're going to the library." The teacher called to the girl from across the park, and she turned to Bill.

"I've got to go. It was good seeing you. Please say a prayer for my sister." And then she was gone.

chapter 17

F riday's sun was still bright and friendly when I
threw my bag into the trunk of the car and pulled
onto the interstate heading for North Carolina.
I'd called her earlier, just to remind her I was coming.
She'd been quick to let me know she didn't need reminding. True to her nature, the next words out of her mouth
were, "Bringing something for the grill?" That made me
laugh out loud, knowing her first thought was dinner. It
would be a quick meal. I was far more interested in
dessert.

The sunlight shone through the passenger side window and beamed down on the box of roses I'd picked
up at the florist before heading for the house, and the
heat was releasing the fragrance into the car even
through the cardboard. I'd gotten a mixture of six red,
six pink, six white, and six yellow. The blooms were as
big as saucers, and I knew she'd be thrilled when they
opened completely, filling the house with the scent even
I liked. After going to the bookstore the day before, I'd
stopped in the pet store next door. The canaries were

chirping and hopping around, and they were cheery and bright yellow. I wanted to bring her one of those too, and I'd called and asked her, "Would you like a surprise?"

"As long as it doesn't have to be fed or walked!" she laughed, ending that idea.

When I left the pet store, I walked a bit farther down to the department store and picked out some diamond earrings. They didn't have to be fed. Flowers and diamonds seemed to be a nice gift combination.

My trip was uneventful, not counting the truck that dropped bales of hay all over the interstate, turning it into an obstacle course. Turning off the main street, then turning again, the car bucked and bumped along Creekside Road, even though I was making a concerted effort to avoid the biggest holes. I swung wide to navigate the new bridge, and honked my horn as I pulled up and back down the crest of the hill. The door flew open and she ran down to the car, straight into my arms. I kissed her, a long, hot kiss. My arms wrapped around her waist, and hers around my neck. She leaned back to look at me. "You look different," she said, puzzled, and I remembered Russ saying the same thing.

"I'm a man in love!" I replied, laughing out loud and lifting her off the ground.

She squealed and laughed, then asked teasingly, "Who do you love?"

"Um, somebody who lives in that house," I grinned, taking her hand and pointing toward the gray clapboards. "And she's really special too, and beautiful and smart.

And she's great in bed." I winked at her, and she winked back. I reached back into the car and pulled out the box of roses. She didn't say a word when she opened it, just smiled and kissed me on the cheek. We climbed the steps holding hands, arms swinging.

Inside, it was plain that something was changed, although I wasn't exactly sure what. It looked different, but I just couldn't decide what the difference was. "Did you do something to the house?" I questioned, looking all around. She was busy putting the flowers in water.

"Can't you see it?" she smiled, pointing to the far corner. Between the fireplace and the corner, hidden from view by one of the wingback chairs, was a desk. It was a stunning mahogany secretary, complete with a leather office desk chair in the same dark green as the wingbacks. It was stocked with gel-tipped pens, note paper, some stationary, and other desk-type things like tape, scissors, paper clips and a letter opener, as well as a brass desk lamp. The blotter and desk accessories were the same dark green leather as the chair. "It's for you. For when you come here, if you need to work on something. It's yours. I bought it the other day in Asheville. Isn't it beautiful?" She gazed at it as one would a fine piece of art.

I had to admit that it was indeed beautiful. It was perfect in every way, not a scratch. If I'd had to guess, I'd have said early eighteen hundreds, and the finest craftsmanship. The chair fit like a glove, soft and comfortable, and I brushed my hand across the glowing wood of the secretary, the grain glistening in the light of the desk lamp. "Do you like it?" she whispered, anxious to receive my approval.

"Diana, it's gorgeous. It's just absolutely . . . well, no one's ever done anything like this for me." That was true. The women I'd dated, lived with, slept with, all wanted gifts and money, cars, clothes, things like that. No one had ever given me anything like this. It was so, well, comfortable. Just like everything about her, about us. I imagined myself sitting here, writing a note to her and putting it on her pillow, or opening mail, but mostly just belonging, having my own space in this house. "I love it, sweetie. I really do. Thank you. Thank you so much. You shouldn't have, but I'm really glad you did."

"My pleasure," she grinned, and leaned down, kissing me quickly and firmly on the lips. "Let's do something about dinner, okay? I'm starved!"

I was getting hungry too. She'd marinated some chicken, laughingly telling me she'd known I wouldn't bring any meat for dinner. We had a fresh salad, complete with little cherry tomatoes and the vinaigrette dressing, and polished off the bottle of blackberry wine she'd opened the week before.

After dinner she treated me to the fashion show created from her trip to Asheville. She had purchased several new dresses, comfortable but shapely floral pieces, and some casual slacks and new polo shirts. There were new shoes too, and jewelry, and bags, and even a hat. I thought it was the silliest-looking thing I'd ever seen, but she loved it, laughing and putting it on me. "Looks great with your hair!" she giggled. My heart sang as I watched her trip and dance about. It felt good to know that someone was excited to see me, just to be with me. That was new for me.

"Ready?" she called from the bedroom after making me wait on the sofa. "Close your eyes. Don't peek!" she ordered, coming back to the living area and leading me down the hall. I bumped into the door facing and then made it through the door before she stopped me. "Okay, you can look now."

I looked at her for just a second, and saw that her whole face was glowing, totally saturated in joy. On the bed behind her were a dozen pieces of lingerie, all colors and kinds. There was a long, slinky, spaghetti-strap dark turquoise gown, and a pair of skimpy red pajamas in bright red stretch lace. Beside the pajamas was a royal blue gown, not too long, the bottom made of satin and the top a stretchy, clingy kind of fabric. She straightened another pair of pajamas, emerald green satin boxers and a button-front top to match. There was a long, white gown too. It had a form-fitting corset-type satin bodice and a sheer, layered skirt, with panties to match. But my favorite was the cat suit lying at the foot of the bed. It was fine black mesh with triple black leather straps on each shoulder and black leather cuffs at the wrists and ankles. The straps were attached to a wide leather band that ran around the top edge of the suit, and leather-covered snaps ran its entire length, all the way down and between the legs, and up the back to the waist. I wanted to see her in that more than any of the others, but I realized she was probably hoping for something a little more romantic.

"Which one?" she asked coyly. I made a big deal out of choosing. I chose the white gown.

"I think I like this one. You'll look like a princess," I said, pointing to it.

She looked shocked. "I was sure you'd like this one best," she exclaimed, pointing to the cat suit.

"You might be right," I laughed, "but humor me, okay?"

She picked the others up and folded them neatly, placing each in its own box, reminding me of the boxes in the window seat, their tissue paper neat and carefully folded. I chuckled to myself as she rearranged the boxes, positioning the one containing the catsuit on the top of the stack. I watched her move, my excitement growing more with each turn of her head, each curling of her fingers. When everything was neatly put away, I sat down on the side of the bed, knees apart, and she stood between them, pulling my face to her neck, her hands locked in my hair. "I'm going into the bathroom," she spoke softly into my crown, kissing the top of my head in the process. "Be ready when I come out, okay?" I was ready, really ready.

The door closed behind her, and I heard her running water in the basin. I took that opportunity to look in the nightstand drawer and found what I'd expected, that the checks were gone. That's how she'd financed the shopping trip. I was glad. She was enjoying the results of her success, even if she took no formal credit. I undressed down to my black satin boxers, a special purchase I'd made for myself. After pulling the elastic band out of my hair, I started to brush it out, and heard the bathroom door open.

If ever I'd wished for a camera, it was at that moment. My arm froze halfway through a brush stroke, and all I could do was stare. The gown fit perfectly, her breasts blossoming out the top. Through the sheer bottom half I could see the tiny panties, almost disappearing against her creamy skin. She turned to light a candle on the dresser, and I put the brush down, sitting down on the bed again, waiting for her to come to me. Climbing onto the bed and crawling across it, she retrieved the brush from the nightstand and, kneeling behind me, began to brush my hair using long, firm strokes. As she brushed, she hummed, and occasionally leaned forward and kissed the side of my neck. I sat perfectly still, not wanting her to stop.

"I've never met a man like you, never made love with a man like you. You're gorgeous. Your skin is like velvet, and you're tender and gentle," she said, her voice honey-drenched and warm, then reached around me, touching me, feeling my hardness. "There are things about you that are stronger, harder, more powerful than I knew a man could be. Do you know how incredible you are?" she asked me, smiling as she tipped my head back and kissed my forehead.

"About half as incredible as you," I grinned, turning around, taking the brush from her hand and dropping it on the floor. My arms wrapped around her waist, and I lowered her to the bed, my lips touching her neck, her chest, her breast, her cheek, anything I could reach. She pulled one leg up and over my back, and ran her hands down my sides. Stopping at my hips, she purred, "Um, new boxers? Nice. Very nice. I've never seen you in boxers."

"You've never seen me in any kind of underwear!" I laughed out loud, and she giggled.

It was like we'd never been apart. But instead of the acrobatics we'd tinkered with the week before, this time I held her close, as close as I could, not wanting to let go, desperate for her arms around me. We rocked together late into the night, her moans soft and urgent in my ear, her lips on my earlobe, my neck, my cheek, my face buried in her hair. When we did part, it was only slightly; I kept my fingers locked behind her back, moving just far enough away to see her face, to kiss her with urgent, hungry kisses. Then I'd slip my hands all the way down her back, gripping her soft bottom and pressing into her again, hard and deep. She would whisper, "More, baby. Don't stop." We'd melt together again, her breasts squeezed against my chest, nipples firm and cherry red. Unlike before, we didn't talk. Words seemed intrusive in the silence. The room was quiet except for our breathing, her moaning, or the whimper I couldn't squelch when I'd filled her again.

There was a current, a flow, when we were together that I'd come to appreciate. It rolled and slipped and slid here and there between us, holding us together in our passion. I could feel it when I touched her, a palpable thing, meandering and lyrical, its own entity. When my hands left her body, they felt drawn again as if there were a magnetic pull, and my palms ached until I pressed them against her flesh again. She felt it too, I could tell, and let it breathe in and out of her, pouring itself into every gap, every crack, every crevice where our bodies didn't meet, following the path of least resistance, binding us together with every stroke, every whispered moan, every touch. I loved that house, that room, that bed, but inside her was my true home.

We fell asleep like that, me inside her, arms tight around each other, her legs firmly around my waist, her neck bent forward, forehead planted against my chest. I remember her hand touching me, her finger tracing the line from my navel up my chest, burying her fingers in the dark hair at my breastbone.

She wouldn't let me out of bed the next morning until we'd come together again, and I remember thinking that everyone should wake up that way each day. After showering and dressing, we ate a light breakfast, and I suggested we drive to Asheville and look around the botanical garden. That was a great idea, she squealed with excitement, and picked out one of the new flowered dresses to wear. I almost decided not to tie my hair back, but she insisted. "There's something so sexy, so intimate, about believing I'm the only one who ever sees it down," she'd said, and I promptly put the elastic back in it, assuring her that she was indeed the only one who saw it down, whose fingers ran through it.

"Let's get to the car," she chuckled, "or we're going to wind up back in bed." She darted out the door with me right behind her.

The garden was beautiful, mostly woodland, and we found a small restaurant down the street for lunch. Our afternoon was spent at a local nursery, where I bought a five-foot-tall cherry tree. "What's that for?" she asked, her eyes squinted slightly.

"You'll see!" I told her, refusing to talk about it further. We stopped on the drive back, tree protruding from the car trunk, and bought junk food, chips and such. She wanted an ice cream sandwich and promptly got it all over her, with no napkin in sight. I found a small gas station, and she washed her hands. When she returned to the car, I had the singular pleasure of kissing the rest of the mess off her face while she giggled and fought me the whole time.

Parking the car in the drive back at the house, I looked at my watch. It was only half-past five, and I lifted the tree out of the trunk. "Got a shovel?" I inquired, and she went around back to find one. When she returned, I said nothing. Taking the shovel and turning, I walked down the slope toward the end of the road.

"Where are you going?" she insisted, following me down the hillside.

"Is this the place?" I asked, turning to her and pointing at the ground.

"What place?" she asked, a little confused by my question.

"The place where we met," I smiled, remembering a pipe shotgun and a deep, firm, feminine voice. One look at her face, and I dropped the tree and the shovel, grabbing her and holding her in a death grip while she heaved and sobbed, a week's worth of pent-up, frightened tears pouring down her face. "Geez, beautiful, you have no idea how crazy I am about you, do you?" I smiled, closing my eyes and sighing as she shook and sniffled.

"I was afraid you'd forget me," she explained, her voice broken and weak. "I was afraid I'd never see you again. I didn't know if you'd come back, if I'd just imagined last week, the things you said to me. I was so scared," she sobbed, her arms around my waist so tight I thought she'd cut me in two.

"No way, never. How could someone who knew you, who loved you, ever forget you?" I grinned, holding her face in my hands, kissing her lightly. "This is our tree. Every time you see it, I want you to think about me. Just keep doing that until . . ." I stopped.

"Until what?" She stopped crying and demanded an answer, her lower lip quaking.

"Until we can do whatever it is we need to do to be together," I said. "I don't know what that is, but we've got to figure it out. It'll work out. I have to believe that."

She picked up the shovel and handed it to me, and I dug the hole. Before I put the tree in, she made me stop. Running back to the house without any explanation, she returned in a few minutes. In her hand she carried the wedding band. Without a word, she dropped it into the hole, and I dropped the tree in on top of it, then filled the hole, tamping down the dirt. If ever I'd doubted our commitment to each other, my doubt was erased in that moment with that one simple act. She watched, silent, and when I had finished, she took my hand and we walked back to the house. On the way to the house, I made my decision: I wanted to grow old with this woman. Even if it meant I shared her with Nick Roberts.

He was being very frugal with the money, only spending it on necessities. It had to last, and he was glad he'd been adding to it. For the time being, he was spending only from what he'd added and hoping he found her before he had to start dipping into the original money.

The grocery store job had fallen by the wayside. He couldn't work and look for Claire. It was a pretty sure bet that she was somewhere there in the city, but it was a big city, and he had no idea where to even start looking. He began by visiting all of the small dress shops; she'd always dressed beautifully, and she might've gone there for a job.

When that rendered no results, he went to shoe stores, then dry goods stores, then dry cleaners and laundries, all with no luck. Taking the trolley was too expensive, so he walked everywhere, and he wondered about Claire. She'd sold her car — was she walking too? He liked to think they were walking around at the same times of day, and that she was looking for him as he was looking for her. It was impossible to believe that they'd never cross paths, even in a city that large.

He'd had his usual lunch — an apple — and was sitting on a bench in the shade of a hickory tree near the street when the trolley stopped a block away. It was a Saturday, and there were great numbers of people out, milling about, shopping, going to the picture shows, or just walking and window shopping. The large crowds split and converged into other large crowds, the colors of their clothing rippling through the masses. The trolley bell clanged and Bill turned to see people climbing aboard. And, even from that distance, he spotted her.

Bill's mind reeled and he jumped from the bench, his crutches clattering to the concrete. Before he could even move he was screaming her name, and he began to run and hop as fast he could on his good leg and bad, pushing people out of the way, a wild look in his eyes and his feet unable to move fast enough. Almost to the trolley stop he spied a little boy with a bunch of daisies in his hands, and he ripped them from the child's fists as he ran past. He shrieked, "Claire! Claire! It's me, Claire! Please, Claire!"

But before he could reach the trolley, it pulled away from the stop and picked up speed. He chased it for two blocks but, of course, never caught it. He wondered, had she heard him? Had she looked out the back of the trolley and seen him, running like a maniac, desperate to reach her? At least he now knew that she took the trolley and a stop that she must sometimes frequent. He'd try there again and, as he made his way slowly back to the bench, a kind elderly gentleman met him and handed him the crutches he'd dropped in his frenzy.

As the trolley pulled away, Claire could've sworn she heard someone calling her name, but Bill hadn't yet cleared the crowd and, as she looked out, she saw no one. It had to be her imagina-

tion after so long in the city with not a soul. There was no one there who knew her. She was alone.

In his room at the boarding house that night, Bill cried himself to sleep. His heart was broken. She'd looked tired and thin. He could fix that if he could just find her.

chapter 18

Sunday's big event, after the morning roll in the hay and my insistence that she dress up, came as a surprise to her. "I haven't forgotten," I promised her, closing the car door, refusing to divulge my plan.

I drove straight to the mall in Asheville, ignoring her questions, changing the subject every chance I got. "The mall?" she said in disbelief, her face screwed into a scowl.

"Wait and see!" I promised with glee, taking her hand and heading toward the main entrance.

"Well, how about this?" I asked playfully, pretending to be surprised. "A photo studio! Wonder what they do here . . ." My voice trailed off as she grabbed me and kissed me in front of dozens of complete strangers, right there in the middle of the mall.

While she chatted with the photographer and looked at backgrounds and props, I went back to the car and brought in a bag of things I'd packed while she was in the shower. There was a pretty floral dress, different from the one she'd worn on Friday evening, and a soft, pastel sweater that matched it. Two other items were a surprise to her: Matching polo shirts I'd picked up the day I'd bought the boxers. "Oh, no," she frowned. "I don't have any jewelry to match these things."

"Well, maybe this will help," I reached into my pocket and pulled out the box holding the earrings I'd bought for her.

She gave me a sheepish smile. "Why, Steve," she grinned, her eyes flirty and bright. "It's not my birthday. What's this all about?" She put them on, and the photographer's assistant declared them the most beautiful diamonds she'd ever seen. I felt like I was ten feet tall, the most charming and good-looking guy on earth. For the first time I could remember I didn't really mind having my picture taken.

Arrangements were made for her to pick out the proofs she liked best and have the photos shipped to the house. "Remember," I said sternly, "I need at least one of you by yourself and one of us together."

"You shall have them," she promised, a fake British accent gracing her statement. I couldn't wait to put one on my desk, to have one beside the bed, to be able to see her even when we weren't together.

We ate at a local Mexican restaurant, and headed back to the house. The conversation was light, pleasant, both of us knowing that I'd have to pack and leave when we arrived at our destination. I pulled the Mercedes into the drive, and she put her hand on the door handle, but didn't open the door. She just sat there. I wondered what she was about to say. It took a minute for her to speak, and when she did it was soft, clear, and to-the-point.

"Steve, where's this relationship going?" There, she'd asked. Now it was my turn, and I didn't have any idea what I wanted to say. I thought a little, and tried to come up with something, anything, that would make sense, afraid that what I really wanted to say was a little premature, or would sound crazy coming from a forty-eight-year-old bachelor.

"I'd say I want to grow old with you, but I think I'm already there," I quipped, growing more uncomfortable by the second.

"Cut the bullshit, Steve. Answer my question." She was insistent.

"Where do you want it to go?" I threw back at her, hoping she'd say something smarter than I had.

"Damn it!" She threw the door open, steam rolling out of her ears. "Damn it. Come up here, bed me down, ask me to share my food, my life, my body, my home. You can't even be serious when it's appropriate. What is this, fun and games? Playing house? Don't you think I deserve an answer?" She was really mad now, and I heard the voice I'd heard that first day with the pipe stuck in the back of my neck. She got out of the car and slammed the door so hard I thought she'd break the window. Turning, she stomped off toward the house, and I jumped out of the car, running behind her. I caught up to her at the steps, blocked her path, and held her shoulders, forcing her to look at me.

"Damn it yourself, Diana! I love you more than I've ever loved a woman, in ways I've never loved any woman." Well, hell, there it was – I'd spent the bank. I felt naked, exposed, ripped open. Everything in me said go for broke, and I headed down that path headfirst. "I've done things with you I've never done with any other woman, said things to you I've never said to any other woman." I was wounded now, bleeding, my heart sticking out. "I can't believe I'm saying any of this, doing any of this. I'm the guy who used women, who threw them away when I'd finished off whatever they had to give. I wish I could tell you how many women I've screwed a couple of times and never called back." I was shaking now, wanting to stop, forcing myself to go on. Her eyes were wide, staring into mine. "I wish you knew how uncomfortable I am with the things I feel for you, how foreign and wonderful they feel, how sorry I am for the years it took me to find you. You can't know. You just can't understand. I feel so foolish, so stupid, so weak. But for the first time in my life, I feel hopeful, like I have some kind of future." My knees were shaking and I sat down on the top step, resting my elbows on my thighs and my face in my hands. She knelt in front of me, looking up into my face. "I didn't plan to fall in love with you. I thought I'd just play around with you for a couple of days and walk away. I never meant to open up to you. I never meant to let you in, to care for you. But I do. I swear I do. I think about you all day, every day. And it's different than anything I've ever known."

"How?" she asked, her eyes curious, brows peaked.

"Because I know, no matter what happens, that we're going to be together. There's this peace, this contentment, I've never felt before. I trust you. And for the first time ever," I said, looking into those eyes I'd come to love and trust, "I don't look at anyone else. I don't think about anyone else. Hell, there's a girl in the copy room I'd been wanting to fuck for months. I walked right past her the other day and didn't even see her. My friends all think I'm nuts." I gave a feeble laugh, and she took my hands.

"What do we need to do? I'll do it. Whatever it is, I'll do it." Her voice was calm and reassuring, and I knew she meant every word.

I took a deep breath and blew it out, trying to relax at least a little. "I need to get through the summer. I've got back-to-back conferences and workshops. By the end of August everything will have settled down, and things will get back to normal. In the meantime, we can talk on the phone every day and make some plans. I've got two more free weekends, and then I'm socked in. Can you handle that?" I asked, my fingers tracing the side of her face, committing its plains and contours, its silkiness, to my memory.

"If I waited six years, don't you think I can wait a few months?" she smiled. "As long as I know we'll be together."

"Forever," I promised, and kissed those lips, the ones that had breathed life back into my heart.

"You just don't work fast enough, Miss Steinmetz. We're going to have to let you go." Claire had heard it before – three times, in fact. She tried to keep up with production, but she was tired all the time.

Her fourth pair of used shoes broke down on her way back to her room at the boarding house. She'd long ago stopped putting on her old saddle oxfords and dreaming. There was no point. Bill would never come. She pulled up her sleeve just enough to look at the tiny fan. It had become a source of great pain for her, something that reminded her of a life she'd never have.

She knew why they'd let her go: She was showing. A single woman in the city and pregnant. No one wanted her. There was no way to make herself a living. And there was one thing she definitely wouldn't do.

She would not go back home. It didn't matter what happened to her, she'd never go back. The hatred, the mental abuse, the emotional torture – she wouldn't be subjected to that ever again. There had to be another way.

When she dragged herself down the stairs that evening to take out her trash, a fancy car covered in chrome pulled up to the curb and a beautiful young woman got out. Her clothes were the finest Claire had ever seen, and she had a fur stole around her neck and was holding a cigarette in a lacquered holder. Jewels dripped from her neck and her ears, and even her satin gloves had jewels around their cuffs. The young pregnant Jewish girl couldn't help but stare. How did people ever have enough money to afford those kinds of things?

"Seen enough?" a voice snapped. Claire turned to see a woman staring at her, cigarette in hand and dress unbuttoned so that the top of her slip showed. "Fancy, huh? Not all of us working girls can earn that kind of money."

"How did she do that?" Claire asked reverently.

"She's a working girl like me. Course, my dates don't usually have that kind of money." The woman smiled, showing a missing upper tooth on one side in the front.

"How do I get a job doing what she's doing?" Claire whispered.

"Oh, honey, it's the oldest profession in the world. Come on. I'll fix you up. Bun in the oven?" she asked.

Claire gave her a blank look.

The woman tried again. "Having a baby?"

"Oh! Yes, yes I am." Claire smiled.

There was a cackle. "Yeah, some customers like that. You should be able to make you a good living that way." She took Claire's hand and led her down the street, straight into hell.

chapter 19

Years earlier, I'd attended a conference for newspaper writers. One of the things they'd drilled into us was the concept of doing writers conferences and workshops. They pointed out the advantages to filling summers with engagements to speak and work with writers. Not only was it a great source of extra income during the summer months, but it gave the speakers plenty of exposure and helped represent their employers in front of potential employees. My boss at the paper thought it was a great idea, so every weekend of every summer I had a conference or workshop to attend, usually Thursday afternoon through Saturday evening. I explained the process to Diana, and she understood. My only break was the last weekend in August, with the last conference scheduled for the weekend of the third week of September. She looked through my planner, and told me she'd plan to come to Knoxville a couple of times during that time to see me, maybe on a Tuesday or Wednesday.

I kept hoping she'd tell me about the book, about Nick Roberts, without me having to ask. I was sure I didn't want to bring it up at that point in the relationship, but I knew we'd have to talk about it eventually. When I asked her about the rug business, she told me it had really grown. There was no evidence anywhere in the house that there really was a rug business, but I said nothing. Testing the waters, I asked her about the room at the end of the hall. "Just what's in there?" I asked her, waiting to see what she'd say.

"It's just storage," she lied. "Just things I don't want to deal with right now." At least that was the truth. I wanted to scream, *I know the truth, I know who Nick Roberts is.* But I didn't.

Leaving wasn't any easier that day than it had been before. She cried, I cried, and she waved as I drove away. I could see her walking toward the tree we'd planted, standing beside it, and wished I'd brought a camera with me.

We talked on the phone every night that week. Then we started e-mailing, but that didn't seem to work as well as hearing that voice, that warmth and passion, on the other end of the phone. I'd call her from the office sometimes too, turning with my back to the window of the main desk, but we'd decided that wasn't a good idea. Once we'd hung up, I couldn't stand up for at least fifteen minutes without embarrassing myself and relating in a very obvious physical way what we'd been talking about on the phone. We limited the phone sex to late

nights, and spent a good deal of our conversational time
planning the next weekend.

It appeared it would revolve around a peculiar event.
Cherilyn had called Diana, wanting to introduce herself
and get to know Diana. Being the hermit that she was,
Diana had asked if she could get together with Cherilyn
sometime when I was around, and that's when Cherilyn
had dropped the bomb. "Oooh, that sounds great!"
she'd squealed into the phone. "Jim and I are having a
big cookout this weekend. Why don't you and Steve
come?" Since it had been Diana's suggestion, she could
hardly refuse, and so Saturday, all day, was committed. I
was a little disappointed, and I could tell she was too.
"It'll be okay," she promised. "After all, we'll have Friday
evening and Sunday afternoon. And we've still got the
nights." Ah, yes, those magical nights. That was enough
to make me agree to the cookout.

We spent the last Friday evening of April in the
house, all over the house, exploring each other further,
both of us trying to find ways to drive the other crazier
than before. We visited the swing in the back yard again,
and found new uses for chocolate syrup and flavored lip
gloss. It was a productive night, mostly producing yawns
the next day while we were trying to pretend we were
enjoying the cookout.

And that cookout was an eye-opener. I saw something I'd never seen before – the new and improved Jim.
By asking the right questions, I discovered Jim hadn't
returned to Knoxville since we'd first come to town.
Instead, he'd hired an attorney to manage the funeral

parlors in Knoxville and was concentrating all his efforts on building one on the property he purchased through Cherilyn.

But there was something more important about the whole arrangement, and that was Jim himself. He seemed so relaxed, so rested. His stutter was gone, and so was his fidgeting, plus he smiled a lot and chatted cordially with the guests, seeming comfortable and completely at ease. Who was this alien, and where was Jim? Finally, when there was a lull in the activities, I just walked over and asked him.

"Steve, it's amazing what a steady supply of good old-fashioned lovemaking can do for a man," he said warmly, slapping me on the shoulder. Then he pointed to Diana and said, "But I see you already know what I'm talking about. You've changed too, Steve. You're in up to your neck, and it's right this time, isn't it? I can tell." He waited for me to confirm that his observations were correct.

"Yes, Jim, I've hung up my bachelor shoes," I smiled, and he shook my hand.

"Congratulations," he offered with a broad grin, his eyes warm and moist. "I'm happy for you guys."

"What about you and Cherilyn?" I asked.

"I've already got the ring picked out," he whispered slyly. I congratulated him too. Michael and Russ had always been so hard on him, but I'd always known that deep down inside Jim was a good, decent guy, just kind of backward and repressed. A good woman had brought out the best in him, and I knew exactly what a relief that was.

We stayed until late that night, and drove back to the house. All I could think about was being alone with Diana and how little time we had left together. I made her promise, as we went into the house, that we wouldn't do anything the next day that we couldn't do naked. She promised me in return that we'd also do some things I didn't know could be done naked, which sounded pretty good to me.

I held her to that promise too. Before I started packing, she ran a tub of hot water, threw in some gardenia bubble bath, and pulled me in with her. I sat in the tub and she sat in front of me, between my legs, lying back against my chest. I wrapped my arms around her, crossing them in the middle, teasing her nipples, and I asked her to show me what she did for amusement when I was gone. Without hesitation, her hands disappeared beneath the surface of the water, and before long her body was stiff, her head resting on top of my left shoulder, convulsing as I pulled and twisted her nipples. After a couple of climaxes, she lay still against me. It was my opportunity. I reached over with my right hand, grabbed her left arm, and turned the inside of her wrist up, exposing the tattoo.

"This is a really seductive piece of artwork. I just love it. But where have I seen it before?" I probed, hoping for an honest answer.

"I don't know," she answered, still unwilling to reveal the secret. "Maybe you've seen it somewhere else, in a movie or something," she offered with a slight shrug.

"I think I remember now," I started over, wondering how she'd react. "I think it was in a magazine. No, I think it was a book. I just can't remember where."

"Hmmm. I don't know. You'll remember it when you least expect." Her voice never wavered. I knew there would be no disclosure.

She lay across the bed, wet and bare, while I packed. When my things were together, I set them by the door and went back to the bedroom. Lying down beside her, I slipped a couple of fingers inside her wetness and stimulated her with my thumb until she came, then offered her a long, hard drink. She jumped on the opportunity with those exquisite lips, her mouth hot and wet, her tongue flicking up and down my shaft as she sucked and licked. I begged her to stop when she'd swallowed at least three times, my muscles tired and sore, and she kissed me deeply. This time she didn't cry. With my fingers locked around a nipple, I kissed her back, smiling at her, knowing she had accepted my love, my heart, everything I had to offer her. When I said, "I've got to go," she got up, pulled on her robe, and followed me to the living area. At the door, I held her tight, kissing her softly for a long, long time. Her arms around me, she tugged the end of my hair.

"See you next weekend?" I asked, knowing the answer.

"I'll be waiting." The confidence in her voice warmed me. She felt secure. That was my greatest desire, to have her know my love and have faith in it. Then she said something that was a revelation to me.

"Steve, what if there were something I really, really wanted to tell you, but I was afraid to? What if it wasn't a very important thing, but keeping the secret would protect you, and us, and our relationship? How would you feel about that? Would you be mad?" She wasn't telling me, but her eyes were. That's why she hadn't told me, to protect us. Did she suspect that I knew? "What if it were something that would tear us apart if it fell into the wrong hands?" I tried to imagine what it would be like if anyone found out who wrote that book, who Nick Roberts really was.

"As long as it didn't have anything to do with infidelity or litigation, I think it would probably be fine," I assured her. "I trust you, Diana. I trust your judgment. I know if there were a secret like that, you'd tell me if you could. Or you'd tell me when it was time. Either way," I repeated, "I trust you." She took my left hand and pressed it to her lips, as though she were repaying a debt of gratitude to me in some way. "I'll see you next Friday night," I added, "and I love you."

"I love you, Steven Joseph Riley. I really do."

She stood in the doorway of the porch as I drove away, still in her robe. I waved, and she waved back. I drove through town on my way back to the interstate, and Jim was sitting in the porch swing hanging in front of Cherilyn's real estate office. I pulled over and put down the car window.

"Headed back?" he inquired, smiling. He walked to the car and leaned down to rest his forearms on the door, his face in the window.

"Yep," I replied. "Gotta go back to work tomorrow."

"Well, be careful," he advised. "We enjoyed having you guys over yesterday. Cherilyn thinks Diana is really nice. You two make a great couple. You seem so, I don't know, in tune with each other."

"I hope so," I said wistfully, wanting him to be right. "See you around."

"Yeah, see you around!" He waved as I drove away. Who would have ever imagined he and I both would find these women in this town?

I thought about what Diana had said as my car hummed down the interstate toward Knoxville. She realized what would happen if anyone found out who authored that book. That's why she hadn't said anything. The inflection in her voice as she'd asked me those questions had told the story of her longing to tell me, but she was worried that the truth would drive us apart. In reality, I knew that it couldn't separate us, but there was that little niggling doubt, knowing what others were capable of. I didn't want to think about it anymore. I just wanted to think about her.

We had one more weekend left, and I wanted it to be the best. When it was over and my conference weekends began, I wanted to be sure of one thing. I wanted to be confident that, beyond a shadow of a doubt, Diana Nicole Frazier belonged to me. I already belonged to her, body and soul. She owned parts of me no other woman had even seen, things I didn't know existed. I wanted her to believe and never doubt that we would be together. I wanted to give her something that would hold her to me until fall, until we could make the big decisions. Finding that thing, that way to cement us together, was my goal for the week.

Bill spent every waking hour looking for Claire. He looked once more in all the places he'd already looked, and then looked in all new ones. Sometimes he didn't come back to the boarding house. He was so far across town from his room that he just slept on a bench on the street and then started looking again.

But he was coming up with nothing. He had no photo of her, so there was nothing for him to show anyone, and her description was that of thousands of young women in the city. It had been seven months and that one glimpse was the only one he'd had of her. It had been his only hope, and that was fading. Even determination wasn't enough. Pretty soon he'd have spent all of the money her father had given him and he'd have to find a job, but it didn't matter. Without Claire, the money meant nothing.

In a dumpy hotel on the south side of the city, men filled the downstairs parlor, smoking and drinking and talking about their sexual escapades. From time to time a woman would come down the stairs and yell, "Next!" The man who'd been waiting the longest would meet her on the stairs and they'd disappear into a room on the second floor.

But some of them came for the woman on the third floor. They'd pass on the other women just to go up there, to have her to themselves for a little while.

So when the next lucky fellow was called up to the third floor, he practically danced up the stairs. When he knocked on the door, a small voice said, "Come in."

He opened the door and there she was: the "Milk Maid." Pregnant ladies of the evening were hard to come by, and when one did come along, they were popular. Claire had never realized that so many men wanted to find a woman they could nurse, and it had kept her busy. Her nipples were sore and swollen, sometimes even chewed, by over-eager customers who just couldn't get enough. Never mind that it wasn't milk — she hadn't delivered yet — they still wanted it. They also loved to have sex with a pregnant woman, treat her roughly, pull and twist her fluid-filled breasts. One man even wanted to milk her like a cow and afterward had taken her from behind, and not in the cleanest way. She'd screamed with pain, but he'd pressed on, and eventually she'd come to realize that men liked that, the dirtiness of it, the illicitness of it, and after that she'd allowed them to do it whenever they wanted. It seemed safer for her baby that way. And when she allowed that, she could see her arm as they pierced her, the fan there, reminding her that the first time had held such joy.

Her baby. Bill's baby. Where was Bill? She wanted him, needed him, prayed every night that she'd find him. But now? Now he'd never want her. She was soiled, damaged, dirty, depraved. Sometimes when those men did things to her she actually liked it and wanted more. But what she really wanted was a human touch, anything to not be alone.

And what would she do with a baby? Would she keep it in a cradle next to the bed where strange men defiled its mother? Allow it to grow up watching them crawl on her, violate her, use her?

Despite her growing belly, she was getting thinner. She had sores in her mouth that she couldn't get rid of. Sometimes when she went to the bathroom she peed blood. There was no money for a doctor, and there was no time. The men lined up all hours of the day and night to use her, and she seldom got more than three hours of sleep out of twenty-four. Her strength was fading and her life was slipping away. And she'd officially lost hope.

chapter 20

The phone rang in my office late Thursday afternoon. It was the desk downstairs.

"Mr. Riley, you have a visitor down here."

"Who is it?" I asked, wondering who would drop by unannounced.

"She won't tell me who she is, but she says you'll be glad to see her." Diana. It had to be Diana, and my feet couldn't move fast enough.

She was standing in the lobby, dressed to the nines in all red with red heels. She'd done something to her hair – maybe rolled it? – and it was chic and sophisticated. Her bag matched her shoes, and she wore a diamond pendant, a single drop from a golden chain. My eyes traveled to her ears. On them were the earrings I'd given her. I thought my heart would burst with joy. I took her hands in mine and gave her lips a light kiss, a promise of things to come.

"Surprised to see me?" she chirped.

"You bet!" I smiled. "Just come for the afternoon?" Inside I screamed, *Oh please, tell me you're staying the night.*

"Nope," she whispered, as though she could hear my thoughts. "I brought a bag to add a day to our weekend. Okay with you if I ride back with you tomorrow?"

"Okay? Wonderful! How'd you get here?" I asked, a bit curious.

"Jim. He had to come in and sign some papers, something to do with one of the funeral parlors. When I found out he was coming in, I asked for a ride. My bag's in his car, and he's taking it to your house and dropping it off." She looked down at her feet, then back up at me. "Could I see your office?"

"Of course. Let me show you around." I knew she was a little less model-like in stature than my old girl-friends, but I wasn't the least bit afraid to introduce her to my coworkers. That was the thing I admired most about her. Diana always looked regal and dignified, even in denim, even when her hair was wild and unruly.

We went up in the elevator to my sixth floor office. Alan, the intern hired to help me during the summer, was standing at the main desk, looking over some features schedules. I introduced Diana, watching the refined way she took his hand when offered, the respect and kindness in her eyes. I was overwhelmed with pride. I took her in my office and shut the door, and I sat down behind the big desk.

"This is great," she exclaimed, looking out the window at the city. "I didn't realize the Advocate was such a big paper."

"Circulation of one hundred twenty-five thousand," I boasted, feeling masculine and important.

"Guess with that glass, we need to be careful what we do in here," she said, still looking out the window.

"Yes, I think so," I smiled, knowing what she was thinking.

"But I guess I could say anything I wanted to you and they couldn't hear us, could they?" she asked innocently. I could feel the front of my slacks getting tight.

"Diana, please . . . Help me out here, okay?" I didn't want to ruin the afternoon. "You're making a great impression on my coworkers. I'm so proud of you. You look fabulous."

"Thanks," she replied, turning to look at me. "I was just playing. I'll save that for later. And by the way, I'm proud of you too. I love you very much. I don't want to do anything that would embarrass you or make you ashamed of me."

"I don't think that's possible, but if you must, you can make up for it later." I grinned at her, and she smiled back. Looking over my desk, she pulled something out of her bag and set it on the credenza against the wall. "Oh, look!" she exclaimed, faking surprise. "What's this?"

It was a picture, one from the photo studio, in our matching polo shirts. She grinned at the camera, and so did I, standing behind her, hands around her waist. Her hands were on mine, and my chin was resting on her shoulder. We were looking at the camera, smiling. I looked up at her, overcome with her presence, and she patted my hand reassuringly.

Jumping up, I grabbed her and kissed her, not caring if anyone at the main desk saw us. She seemed startled at first, then put her hands on my hips and kissed me back. We stood like that, in our own little world, for several minutes. I heard a sound, like a crowd in a baseball stadium, so I pulled away from her and looked through the interior windows. In the big room outside my office, the whole features crew stood, watching us, and they were clapping and cheering. "Your face is as red as my dress!" she laughed, and I laughed too, then waved at them. They were all smiling, some waving, some still clapping. People I barely knew, some I thought disliked me, were happy for me, for us. Diana reached up to wipe a smudge of lipstick from my lower lip, and I kissed her fingers. *A dinner party would be good*, I thought, a great way to introduce her to people I knew. I'd have to talk to her about that. I wanted to show her off, show her how much I admired her.

The clock above my doorway said four o'clock, and I gathered up a few papers before we left. In the hallway on the way to the elevator we ran into my boss, Richard. I introduced them quickly, wanting to get to my place as soon as possible, to be alone with her.

"Diana, this is our chief features editor, Richard Robbins." She extended her hand. "Richard, this is my friend, Ms. Frazier." He took the hand she'd offered in both of his and gave it a gentle squeeze.

"It's a pleasure to meet you, Ms. Frazier. I trust you're the one responsible for Steve's amazing change in attitude and disposition!" His laugh lines wrinkled and he gave her a broad smile.

"It's Diana, please. And I'd like to take credit for that, but it doesn't all belong to me. He was a pretty great guy to start with," she grinned, patting me on the shoulder.

"Are we talking about a different guy?" he ask, chuckling. "You'd better hang onto her, man. She's a keeper! Nice to meet you, Ms. Frazier." He waved as he headed back into the features department. I wanted to sing, to point at her and tell everyone, *Hey, look, everyone! This is my woman. Isn't she great?* But I knew she'd never go for the singing.

I drove to Lincoln Crossing, thinking we'd have dinner. The urge welled up inside me to blurt out, *This is where it all started. This is where the search began that ended at that little clapboard house on Creekside Road.* But I couldn't. We pulled into the parking lot, and she asked firmly, "What are we doing here?"

"Aren't you hungry?" I asked.

"Not for food," she said, a sense of urgency in her voice. "I want you. That's all. Steve, I'm dying inside without you. Please, let's just go to your house. Please?" Why was I worrying about eating when she was begging to be alone with me? I pulled out on the street and made it home in record time.

We christened my bed several times, then slept fitfully. She was still asleep when I left for work on Friday morning. I called home at lunchtime and found she was watching TV, something she couldn't do at her place.

"There's so much stuff on here that I didn't know about," she said. I told her where to find some fresh vegetables and fruit for lunch. She'd found it, she said, and was thinking about taking a nap. When I came in from work, I woke her and she helped me pack to go back to North Carolina.

The weekend was bittersweet, both of us knowing it was the last for awhile. We never left the house, glued together in every way we could think of. I didn't want to think about the next few months, how lonely they'd be, how far away she'd be. At times we were desperate and depraved, begging each other for one more touch, one more kiss, one more taste of heaven. At others, we were overwhelmed with the peace I'd come to know, celebrating the security we both felt in each other's affections. More than anything, we talked, about our passion, about our love, about our bodies and how they felt together.

One last time, as I pushed hard and deep inside her, I pressed my hand into her abdomen, feeling that movement, that togetherness, knowing it was me and her. I grabbed her hand and, pressing it where mine had been, I covered it with my own hand and pushed into her again, powerful enough that I could feel it even through her hand. "Feel that?" I whispered to her, unable to hold back the tears any longer. "Remember how that feels. Don't forget it. That's us, Diana. That's us together. Think about that every time you miss me. Four months isn't that long." I wished I could convince myself of that, but it seemed like an eternity to us. She pulled my face to hers and kissed me, but I couldn't stand it, couldn't contain it. I stretched out on top of her, my arms around her, and sobbed out loud, all the love and pain and fear and joy wrapped up together in my embrace. Her tears were silent, but they filled her eyes and ran down her cheeks, falling into her hair and wetting it, wetting my hair too. I was home, and I didn't want to leave.

Later that afternoon, I drove up the crest of the hill one last time for four months – a third of a year. I drove slowly, the window down, waving and blowing kisses, watching her standing on the steps, trying hard to be brave. I topped the hill and started down the other side, tears blurring my vision. Stopping at the bottom of the hill, just before the bridge, I wiped my eyes. That's when I heard it, a sound I hoped I'd never cause again.

It was Diana, wailing as I'd never heard a woman cry, the sound of fear, of complete and utter anguish, the sound of a heart broken, piercing my ears, slashing my soul to ribbons. It echoed in my head all the way back to Knoxville. I heard it in my dreams. It wouldn't go away. It had nowhere to go.

Anyone looking at Bill McInnes would think that he was much older than his twenty-seven years. He was gaunt, his eyes and cheeks were sunken, and his limp was much worse than it had ever been. Even his crutches were bowed and almost broken.

His job at the newest grocery in town had given him an income that was enough to afford a nicer room in the south end of town. Many other single people worked in that area, and he made some friends, especially a couple of young men from the local university, working their way through college. They sometimes invited him to come with them for a beer, and he always enjoyed that. But when they asked him, "Hey, McInnes, why always so sad?" he had nothing to say to them.

Leaving a bar one night, the youngest man, Joe, said, "Hey! Let's go have some fun. I'm in the mood for a little lovin'." Bill let them lead him down the street to the closest house of ill repute. Once they'd settled into the parlor, it wasn't long before Joe and Herschel, the other young man, had made their way up the stairs with an available woman.

The madam took a look at Bill. "Cripple, huh?"

Bill smiled. "War wound."

"Hmmm." She looked around furtively, then leaned to his ear. "We've got a special treat on the third floor. She's usually more, but nobody's had the money tonight. I'll give you a trip up there for the regular price if you can make it up the stairs. Better hurry, though – she's going fast!" she laughed.

Bill managed to get to the third floor and knocked on the door. "Come in," a weak voice said.

The room was dark and Bill could barely see, but he could make out a form in the bed. "I'm sorry, I'm having trouble getting oriented because it's so dark."

"Too bad. I don't like working in the light. You want it, you can find it. How do you want it? Front door? Back door? Sorry, I can't use my mouth these days, so if that's what you want, you'll have to go to someone else."

"No, no, that's all right." He tried to get a good look at her, but her back was to him. "I suppose behind would be all right." He watched her struggle to get up on her hands and knees, and

that was when he realized — she was pregnant. "Oh, my god, you're with child!"

She laughed, and he remembered Claire's laugh, that sound like bells. "Girl's gotta make a living some way. You can milk me if you want. Whatever you want." She wheezed. "Get to it. I don't have all night. Time is money."

Bill dropped his trousers and took his place behind her. As he pressed into her, she didn't make a sound, and he wondered how many times a day men plied her flesh that way. His hands gripped her hips, their bones prominent, then wandered up her back, feeling her ribs through her skin. He stroked around her sides, feeling her large, hard belly as it hung full and ready. Without thinking, he asked, "How much longer before your baby comes?"

"Any day," she answered back in a grunt. "'Bout done back there?"

"No. I'm having trouble, I think." He had been working for his satisfaction for ten minutes, but he couldn't seem to get to the point of no return. It all seemed so sordid and filthy to him that he was having problems.

"Would it help if I groaned like I was enjoying it?" she asked.

"No, I don't think so, but thanks. I'll try to hurry." He began a vigorous motion and finally climaxed, then removed himself from her body and stood. "Thank you for that," he said, not knowing exactly what one said to a prostitute whose body he'd just taken.

"You're welcome. You have a nice evening, sir," she said and lay back down heavily.

On his return to the boarding house, Bill washed himself thoroughly and went to bed. She was the first woman he'd been with since Claire, and he hadn't even been able to see her face.

Or the tiny tattoo on her arm.

chapter 21

Aching for her day in and day out became a way of life. We spoke every day on the phone, and every time I heard her voice I felt that stirring, that hope. Most of our conversations were spent talking about the fall, what we'd do together, the places we'd go, the time we'd spend together, the decisions we'd make. We reserved the physical talk for late night calls. She realized one moan from her, even over the phone, would set me off, and she used it mightily.

The conference season started with a bang. It began with a writers' workshop in Charleston the second weekend in May. The following weekend I flew to Fort Lauderdale for a workshop, with the added bonus of being the keynote speaker. Diana said the only way she could've been more proud of me would've been if she were there to hear me herself.

Following those, there was a national newspaper writers' conference in Dallas, followed by two more workshops, one in Philadelphia, the other in Las Vegas.

"Don't sleep with a showgirl," Diana had giggled.

"You're the best show in town!" I'd laughingly assured her.

I did Detroit, Chicago, and Minneapolis-St. Paul on three successive weekends. "You're beginning to sound like a Yank," she teased. I knew there was no chance that would ever happen.

In between, I worked furiously to get my features done, having little time for research, passing most of that on to Alan. Diana and I talked on the phone every evening I was in Knoxville, which was just during the week, but during the conferences, I spent so much time schmoozing and networking with writers and would-be writers that I dropped exhausted into bed every night. We planned our lives, it seemed, around that free weekend at the end of August. I was desperate to see her. More than once I asked her, "Why don't you come up during the week and spend a couple of days?" And every time, sensible creature that she was, she responded, "Because you have your regular work to do during the week, don't you? Please, Steve, I want to wait until we can be together with no distractions, okay?" She wanted me to do what was right, to do my best. I couldn't fault her for that, but I missed her, everything about her, so much that I hurt. All I wanted to do was see her, hold her.

But I got a great opportunity at the expense of enormous disappointment. Richard called me into his office the second week of July. He was acting rather peculiar as he told me to come in, sit down, and close the door. I assumed something was wrong. He started by asking me if I had a weekend free in August.

"Yes," I answered quickly. "I don't have a conference the last weekend in August. Why?" I queried. I knew he'd seen my schedule. I'd copied it to him myself.

"Great," he replied. "I got word that the Secretary of State and the governor will be here that weekend. There's going to be a huge unveiling ceremony for a monument in town, the statue of that war general." I knew he meant General Knox, one of the founders of what we knew as Knoxville.

"Why are you telling me this?" I inquired. "Isn't that something for the news desk? I mean, it's the unveiling of a statue." Diana's face flashed in my mind, and I felt our plans crumbling around me.

"It seems the Secretary of State has twelve children, eight of whom are adopted foster children. Of the eight, three are handicapped, and one has AIDS. I've spoken to the State Department, and we've been granted an interview to do a human interest story. They've seen your work and they're all for it. Of course, you'll have to work with the Secret Service on the details, and there'll be a lot of research required to get some background on the guy. This is a great opportunity, Steve. You could be the star at this year's awards banquets, all of them. You in?"

My heart sank. This was the moment every journalist dreams of, begs for, hopes for, pins a star to. Future book deals, bigger jobs, everything rode on this interview, this story. Diana would be so proud. She would understand, would want me to do it. I knew it would be okay. After all, what was a few more weeks? We'd get by somehow.

"Sure, Richard. You bet. I'm ready." We rose and he shook my hand. "Good luck," he smiled, slapping me on the shoulder. Now I had to find some way to break the news to Diana.

I told her that night on the phone. At first she was quiet, and then, in her best fake-cheerful voice, gushed, "Congratulations, sweetheart! You'll do a great job. I'm really excited for you. I can't wait to see the article." A voice inside me whispered, *I'd like to be half as successful as you,* but I wasn't ready to let her know I was aware of Nick Roberts' identity. I was still grappling with a way to explain to her how I had come to be on her property in the first place.

"It's going to be okay, angel. You'll see. It's just a few more weeks. Just think how crazy we'll be for each other by then."

"Yeah, just a few more weeks," she mimicked, trying to convince herself. I heard her sigh. "It'll be okay."

A few days later, I called Jim, who had moved in with Cherilyn. "Have you seen Diana?" I asked, anxious to know that she really was fine.

"No, as a matter of fact, I haven't," he admitted. "Cherilyn asked her to come down and visit, but she said she'd been working around the house and was really tired. I haven't seen her at all. Why?"

"Just wondering. We haven't been able to see each other . . ."

"Conference season, huh?" he asked, knowing the answer.

"Yeah. I was just a little concerned about her. I'm sure she's fine. We talk every night, but I just want to be with her so much, you know? I miss her." I hoped he couldn't hear the agony in my voice.

"I can't imagine how you can stand it," he offered, extending sympathy. "I couldn't stand to be away from Cherilyn. We haven't announced it yet," he whispered into the phone, "but we got married last week."

"Congratulations! That's great! I'm really happy for you both!" I wanted to scream, to die, to run to the car and drive to North Carolina. All I could do was congratulate my friend, wish him well, and envy him. What was I doing, sacrificing something so dear and precious for a damn job? I kept telling myself it was only temporary.

The day of the interview loomed closer. I received a packet of information from the Secret Service and some forms to fill out, with more for Richard and the owner of the paper to fill out and sign. I had to find a cameraman and arrange for a good sound system and technician to tape the interview. They made publicity shots of me for the Secret Service to forward to the White House, and to keep on file for identification purposes. There was still my regular work to be done and, on top of that, one conference right after another. I was exhausted most of the time, and Diana could tell. She told me over and over, "You need to rest, and I need you. Cancel a conference and come up here, please? You need a break." I couldn't. The momentum was building, and I was riding the crest of the wave, that thing I'd been taught to do, groomed to do, for years. There was something exhilarating within the exhaustion. I missed her, but I knew she'd be there, waiting. Her voice kept me going. I hoped I was doing the same for her.

I came back from a four day, Thursday-through-Sunday conference in Phoenix and called Diana as soon as I walked through the door. Something wasn't right, I could tell.

"Hello?" she answered so softly I could barely hear her.

"Hi!" I said, trying to sound as bright and cheerful as possible. "What's going on around there?"

Her voice was strained. "I can't talk right now." I could hear some kind of noise in the background, like a hammer or something being beaten rapidly.

"What's wrong?" I demanded, my chest tightening, my pulse growing more rapid.

"Steve, please, I can't talk right now." I felt my panic growing.

"Diana, please, I know something's wrong. I'll come right now, okay? I'll be there in a few hours."

"No!" she insisted, her whisper firm. "No, Steve. Don't come. Stay there. Please. I'll call you tomorrow night. I've got to go. I love you, but I've got to go."

"But I won't be here . . ." I tried to tell her, but she'd hung up. I called Jim and Cherilyn, but no one answered at Cherilyn's house. I was nauseous, frightened for her. I fought down pure terror, telling myself that she would call back soon. I didn't sleep, just tossed and turned, wanting desperately to go to her, and wanting to honor her wishes.

The interview was scheduled for Friday afternoon. My pager went off on Monday morning in the car on the way to the office. I looked at the screen: Russ. I'd call him later. I had a full day, a deadline to meet, and preparations to be made for the interview, not to mention the sick feeling I had in my gut over Diana and the way she'd sounded the night before. Retreating to my office as soon as I hit the sixth floor, I pulled a couple of stacks of paperwork together and grabbed a pen, working furiously. I hadn't even noticed the people on the features department main desk. They were congregating in small groups, talking and looking at something. My phone rang.

"Mr. Riley, it's a Mr. Russell for you on three." I thanked the operator and picked up the phone.

"What, Russ? This had better be good. I'm really busy."

"Steve, it's about that book . . ."

"What book?" I barked, irritated at him and the piles of paperwork in front of me.

"*The Celtic Fan.* Have you . . ."

"Russ, I really don't have time for this right now. I'm up to my neck in paperwork and my whole career hinges on Friday. Can't this wait?"

"Well, not really, Steve. About the book, I think you should . . ."

Just then, Richard opened the door to my office. "Russ, I've gotta go. My boss is here."

"But Steve, this is really important. Please, you need to . . ."

"Bye, Russ." I hung up the phone and looked at Richard. "I'm sorry. A friend. What's up?"

"Have you seen this," he said, grinning. "They've done it. The Asheville Examiner scooped the story. It's all over the TV and Internet now." He tossed the first section of the Examiner on my desk. That's when I noticed everyone in the features department talking, buzzing, pointing at newspapers all over the room and staring at the news feed.

I picked up the paper and turned it around. There was a fuzzy, digitally-enhanced picture on the front page of a woman at what looked like a teller's window. The caption read, "This photo, taken from a bank security camera, led an Examiner reporter to the truth about the author as she cashed checks made out to her pseudonym." I looked at the headline. Its bold letters leaped off the page: "Author revealed: Small-town widow the real Nick Roberts." That's when I saw the other photo, small and in the bottom corner of the page. Underneath it was the caption, "The author in front of her home in Ebbs Mill. She refuses to comment on the book or its subject matter." I looked at the photo. It was Diana. She was standing at the end of the driveway on the bridge. Although she was looking at the camera, the shot hit her sideways, and the look of fear and confusion in her eyes knocked the breath out of me. I looked closer, and began to feel the walls close in, the air being sucked out of the room. There was something about the photo, something

I almost hadn't noticed but, knowing her the way I did, it was unmistakeable. A metallic taste came up in my mouth, and my heart stopped beating. The picture didn't lie. It was plain as day.

She was pregnant. Her tummy protruded, round and full, not extremely big, but very obvious, at least to me.

I don't remember much after that. When I turned to look at the picture of us together on the credenza, Richard's face paled as he realized who she was.

"Steve, my god, man, I'm sorry. I didn't realize . . ."

My chair hit the floor as I jumped out of it, knocking papers off the desk, paperclips and pens going everywhere. I couldn't think, couldn't hear what was going on around me. All I could think about was Diana, alone and scared, needing me, trying to tell me, praying I would come back. I'd let her down, left her vulnerable and terrified. The exhaustion I'd heard was from carrying my child, the thing she'd wanted to share with me. And I guessed the noise in the background the night before had been news crews and reporters banging on the door. I flew through my office door and headed for the hallway. I punched the elevator button a couple of times, but couldn't just stand there and wait. Heading for the stairs, one of the features crew, a young woman named Bethany, called out, "Hey, Steve! Hear about Nick Roberts?" I took the stairs three at a time, hit the ground running, and was in my car and out of the garage, tires screeching, heading for the interstate. She was alone. She needed me. And I wasn't there.

The accelerator was pressed all the way to the floorboard, and I did everything I could to coax a few more miles per hour out of the engine. Fishing in the mess on the front seat, I found my cell phone. I dialed her number three times, each time pushing at least one digit wrong, having to start over, hands shaking. Busy; she probably had it off the hook. Voicemail on her cell; most likely turned off. I wanted to hear her voice, needed to tell her how sorry I was, how much she meant to me. Most of all, I wanted her to know that I didn't care about Nick Roberts, or the stupid book, or the interview, or the conferences. None of that mattered anymore. All that mattered was the angel with golden hair, sitting on the old porch swing, strumming the strings of a mysterious instrument and singing, the sun shining on her face in the clear spring air.

He'd given up. Claire was not going to be found. Bill lived each day in a haze, trying to figure out what to do with the rest of his life. Without her, it seemed useless. Working, drinking, sleeping, eating, it was all a waste of time.

He couldn't hear Claire's wails a few blocks away as the child he'd planted in her womb made its way into the world, screaming bloody murder. "That baby's not gonna keep you from doing your job, is it? Because if it is, she or the both of you will have to go."

"No, no ma'am, I'll work it out." Claire held the tiny infant to her breast, and all the months of having men abuse them paid off. Her nipples were large and hard, and the baby latched on

immediately, drinking deeply. She smiled down at the tiny child, its hair a lighter shade than her own, its features decidedly not Jewish.

"What should I name you?" she whispered. "I'll name you Tikvah." The baby gurgled and grinned. "It means hope." That was important to Claire. If her child didn't at least have hope in her name, she'd have none at all.

chapⲦⲈR 22

Gravel flew as my tires hit the narrow road. Looking back in my rearview mirror, I saw a van belonging to a national network television affiliate from an Asheville TV station coming up behind me. Furious, I waited until I reached the three houses before hers and cut my wheels, sending my car sliding sideways in the loose rocks. When it stopped, I threw it in park and jumped out. The driver of the van looked surprised. "Move your damn car, buddy!" he shouted, honking his horn.

"Leave us alone!" I hurled a large rock at his windshield with considerable force, heard the satisfying *thud*, saw the cracking of the glass.

He put down his window and stuck his head out. "Hey, what the fuck, man?" he screamed at me, but I didn't turn. I had taken off running down the road toward the house. At the end of the driveway, on the new bridge, I could see close to a dozen cars, with at least one sheriff's deputy in the midst, his lights flashing. As I neared the bridge, I heard a female voice shrill,

"There he is! That's the guy I was telling you about. He's the father of her baby." It was Cherilyn, and the reporter she was yapping to was Art Washburn, a long-time associate of mine from the Asheville Examiner. He looked directly at me, and his jaw dropped a foot.

"Steve? Steve Riley? Is that you?" Ignoring his question, I turned to Cherilyn; I know I looked like a maniac, with my face burning and eyes surely ablaze.

"Cherilyn, you damn media whore! Shut up!" I looked around. "All of you, get out of here! Leave! Leave us alone!" I started across the bridge and felt a hand grab my arm, pulling me back. The sheriff's deputy spun me around and looked me in the eye. The wildness in my eyes wouldn't go away; I could feel it, tell he was wondering what my problem was.

"I need to see some form of identification, sir," he said calmly, pointing to my back pocket. I took out my wallet and handed it to him. When both his hands were occupied with my wallet, I took off at a dead run up the hill. I heard him yell, "Stop! I order you to halt!" I heard the click of a hammer on a handgun, but it didn't matter. I couldn't stop. I was too close.

Then Cherilyn's voice cut through the chaos, and she yelled, "No! Don't shoot! He's okay, let him go!" I cleared the crest of the hill, my lungs bursting, the house in sight. I wanted to thank Cherilyn and take back what I'd said to her, but that wasn't important, not right at that moment. All I wanted to do was get to Diana.

I hit the porch, slid into the door, and tried the knob. Pounding the wood, I screamed and pleaded, "Diana!

Diana! Please, it's Steve! Please, let me in!" I crumpled to the floor in front of the door, babbling and crying, incoherent, uncomprehending, unable to move. Above me, I heard the "click" of the lock, and the door opened just a crack, then swung wide.

In an instant I was in her arms, her lips against my cheek. I cupped her face in my hands and stared into those eyes, dancing eyes, warm and smiling, filled with tears and love, a combination I couldn't lose, couldn't walk away from again. She pulled me inside and closed the door behind me, locking it. I tried to speak, but words wouldn't come, and she put her finger to my lips to calm me. She turned with her shoulder blades against my chest and drew my arms around her, holding the backs of my hands in her palms. Placing my palms just under her collarbone, she ran my hands down her body. As they passed over her breasts, I could tell they were larger, full and tight, swollen with fluid, and she gasped slightly as I touched her nipples. I closed my eyes, resting my chin on her shoulder, and she continued downward. They moved under her breasts, and I lifted up slightly, feeling their weight, the heaviness, wondering how tired her shoulders were at the end of the day, reminding myself to give her a good backrub. She turned my wrists and drew my hands downward. They immediately began to move forward, over the place where her slim waist used to be, out farther and farther, until they stopped even with her navel. Her skin under the cotton dress was tight, and I spread my fingers wide, taking in the size of her tummy, the width, the depth, moving around it like gripping a basketball. And then it happened.

It kicked, a good, hard kick. I could feel it rolling around inside her, stretching and moving, moving deep in her as I had just a few months before on that first night, asking her how it felt to carry a child inside her. I remembered, and she was right. It did feel the very same. My moving inside her had created this movement, and I bit my lip to keep from crying out, from shouting, from wailing in joy as I'd heard her wail in sorrow. She pivoted in my arms and stared into my face, her eyes sad, pain an inch thick over her expression.

"Steve, I wanted to tell you, really I did. I wanted to tell you about the baby. And I wanted to tell you about . . ."

I put my hand up to quiet her. "I knew, Diana. I already knew." She looked at me, puzzled. I drew her over to the sofa and sat down beside her. "Remember when we first met?" She nodded. "Well, I lied. The real reason we were here was to look for Nick Roberts." She was still, quiet, waiting for the rest of the explanation. "When I first came here, I was looking for Nick Roberts. Before I left here the first time, I knew you'd written that book. But I didn't say anything because by that time I didn't care. I came to find Nick Roberts. What I found was a beautiful woman, the love of my life. Nick Roberts and anything associated with Nick Roberts just didn't matter anymore."

"Why didn't you tell me you knew?" she asked, looking down at her hands, unable to meet my eyes.

"Because. Because it didn't matter. Because I knew I'd have to explain to you why I was here in the first place. Because I was afraid you'd be afraid, afraid I was just playing you, afraid I'd expose you and give you up to the media. But I didn't, I swear to god. It wasn't me."

"I know," she said, finally looking at me, relief washing across her face. "It was me. I'm the one who did it. I took the checks from New Century to the bank, and one of the clerks noticed the name of the payer. She talked the bank manager into matching the time and date of the deposits with the video cameras, and then gave the photos to the reporter from the Examiner, and he did the rest. It was all my fault."

"Why, baby? You knew what would happen. Why would you do that?"

Her tear-filled eyes looked up into mine. "I wanted to cash those checks and deposit the money. I wanted to send you a copy of my bank statement to show you that you didn't have to work there unless you wanted to."

"Aw, honey, you didn't have to . . ."

"But I'm glad it's over, really. I just don't know what to do now." She looked so tired, so small, her little round belly resting on her legs.

I pulled her to me and held her as tightly as I could. "What do you want me to do, Diana? I'll do anything you want me to."

In her usual fashion, she simply said, "What do you think you should do, Steve? What will be best for you? What do you want?" A spark of realization passed over her face. "My god!" she cried out. "You're missing the interview! Steve, what were you thinking!"

"I was thinking about you. Nothing, no one else. Just you. Both of you." I knelt in front of her, unbuttoned the three buttons halfway down her dress, and drew it open, kissing her tummy. I felt her reach behind my head and pull the elastic band out of my hair, running her fingers through it to free it. "Nothing else matters anymore. The job, the career, the money. Nothing else. I want to be here. This is my home." My tears dripped into her lap, and I pressed my cheek against her belly, feeling the baby moving slowly. "When I draw my last breath, I want it to be in this house, with you, right back there in that bed, with our children gathered around. That's what I want."

In her matter-of-fact tone, she pulled my face up to meet hers and asked me again, "So what do we do about it? How do we resolve this?"

"What do you want me to do, Diana? I'll give you anything, do anything you want."

"Right this minute?" she quipped, her mischievous smile returning.

"Right this minute. Anything you want."

"I want you to promise me that you're mine from now on," she said firmly. "I don't want to share you with anyone but this baby. I don't want you to go back to the city. I don't want you to leave me. I don't want you to love any other woman but me." Her voice was tightening. "I want you to tell me you'll love me forever, and promise that won't change."

I reached into my pocket and pulled out the little box. Snapping it open, I placed the ring I'd purchased weeks before on her finger and watched her eyes light up like the stone on her hand, shiny, full of hope and promise. "And I want you to change your last name to Riley. What do you say to that?" I asked breathlessly, sure of the answer, my hands sweating and heart throbbing.

"I'd say that's exactly what I had in mind. If you don't mind your bride being as big as a house, it won't bother me!" She kissed me, one of those soft, hungry kisses, full of longing.

"You won't be that big. It'll be so soon that no one will notice in the pictures except us. Now, anything else, Mrs. Riley?"

"Yes. Make love to me, right now. I can't wait another minute." She saw the look of alarm on my face. "Oh, I bet you've never been with a pregnant woman, have you?" She grinned as I shook my head.

"Any special instructions?" I asked as she led me down the hall, pausing to open that locked door, to fling it open, to let out the ghosts that had lived there too long. She pulled me onto the bed and said, "Only three. Slow, sweet, and all night long. Think you can handle that?"

"No doubt in my mind," I chuckled, wiping a drop of moisture from her nipple and licking my finger.

Inside her, everything was right again, and for the first time in weeks my heart stopped aching. I slid my entire length into her, and the baby rolled and kicked. I could feel it moving against my hardness, complaining, angry that its space was being invaded, unhappy to share its mom with me. When Diana realized I could feel it, she started to laugh. "Tell him you were here first, Dad!" she squealed, and I started laughing too. Our lovemaking dissolved into peals of laughter, the laughter of two extremely relieved people who knew the hurdles had been cleared. I'd never wanted her as much as I wanted her right at that moment, her breasts full and tight, the baby squirming inside her, a child we'd made together. Every hope, prayer, wish, dream I'd ever had, they all came true in that moment. Most people search all their lives for the illusion of happiness, but I'd found the real thing.

When we stilled and lay together in the darkness, she asked me quietly, "What now, Steve? What are you going to do?"

"First things first. I'm going to marry Diana Frazier," I teased. "She's carrying my baby, you know."

"But your job," she protested, "and your house . . ."

"This is my home," I reminded her. "No matter what." I stopped and thought for a minute. "What would Bill and Claire have done."

"If Bill had the opportunity, he'd do everything differently. He'd do it right."

"And so shall we." Like all the times before, I kissed her and then held her as she lay beside me, her head on my shoulder, our bodies wrapped together in a huge knot, my fingers caressing her nipple. She fell asleep before I did, the rhythm of her breathing calming me as the baby moved and turned, a part of me still inside her.

The men left the bar and wandered up and down the streets. "Hey, want to have some more fun?" Herschel asked as they neared the whore house.

Bill thought back to the pregnant woman. "No. That's okay. If you guys want to, go ahead. I'll just wait downstairs for you."

"Hey, what's going on over there?" Joe asked. A crowd was gathered on the sidewalk in front of the building, whispering and pointing. As they neared, Bill asked a bystander, "What's this about?"

"Whore threw herself out the third floor window."

"Is she dead?" Bill asked in horror.

"Of course!" The man laughed and walked away.

The third floor. The woman he'd purchased for his pleasure. He pressed his way through the crowd to find her body lying on the sidewalk, a pool of dark red blood under her head, her vacant eyes staring up at the sky. "Can someone please get a sheet to cover her with?" he cried out. Someone from the building threw one out the upstairs window, and with the window open, he could hear a baby crying.

He did his best to straighten up her arms and legs and pull her night dress down to cover her immodesty. Before he drew the sheet up, he decided her arms should be folded with her hands on her chest, and he took her left arm in his hand, lifting it up inadvertently into the light.

And there it was – the tiny fan tattoo.

Bill's stomach turned and his heart threatened to stop. Everything was churning, his gut, his vision, the concrete sidewalk around him, all heaving and unstable. He tried to scream, but nothing came out, and he wanted to cry, but he couldn't. All he could do was kneel on the concrete by her body, holding her hand.

A woman came out of the building, barely clothed, and said, "Well, damn, a dead whore to bury. I wish I knew who her people were and I'd send her body to them to take care of."

Bill stood and straightened, his eyes filling and burning. "May I have a pencil and paper, please?" The woman motioned him inside. She handed it to him and he wrote something on it, tears falling on it like warm summer rain, then handed it back. When she opened it, it read: *Claire Steinmetz, Madison Street, Pine Grove. I told you one day you'd regret it.*

chapter 23

We gathered on the crest of the hill, me, Diana, Jim, and Cherilyn, to whom I'd apologized over and over, thanking her for saving my life. She'd explained that she was only talking to the media because, as she put it, "It's better to hear things like that from a friend than some jealous, nosy bastard who hates you and will tell damn lies about you." She sounded like she knew what she was talking about. I couldn't argue with that logic anyway.

The minister brought his wife and, along with the four of us, they stood at the top of the hill. We repeated the words he told us, and Diana said "I do" in a strong, clear voice. Part of the ceremony I spent holding her hand, and part of it with my hand on her middle, wanting him to be included. When the minister asked me to kiss her, Jim and Cherilyn clapped and cheered for the longest time, then Cherilyn kissed and hugged Diana, kissed and hugged me, kissed and hugged the minister, kissed and hugged everybody, after which she announced that ours would have a playmate by the following spring.

Jim was a changed man. Before they left, the minister asked me if he could do anything else for us. I turned to our guests and simply said, "I want you to see something special, something that changed my life forever." I took my wife's hand and led her to that old porch swing. Placing the Tennessee music box in her lap, I walked down the crest of the hill and over toward the end of the road, stopping just down the other side of the hill, far enough that I could see over it. I leaned gently against the tree we'd planted, and they joined me there.

And there we stood, as I had months before, watching a beautiful woman with golden hair strum an ancient instrument and sing in a voice pure and bright, her notes floating upward, carrying my heart aloft.

He held the little girl's hand and made his way across the cemetery, his brace and cane helping him along. His wife walked with them as he took in the familiar landscape. "Did I ever tell you about your great-grandmother, Marcy?"

"No, Grandpa Bill."

"Well, she was a beautiful lady, very beautiful. Her name was Claire. She was my first true love," he said, his voice coarse with age.

"Did she have dark hair like me?" the little girl asked.

"She did! And big dark eyes like your mama's and grandma's. Your Grandma Hope is her little girl, you know."

"My grandma was a little girl?" the child laughed, her eyes sparkling.

"Long time ago she was! I wasn't there when she was born, but I took her home with me not too long after. She was a pretty little thing, had her mama's eyes and my hair. But then when your mama came along, she had the same dark hair and eyes as my Claire."

"That's cool, Grandpa Bill. Can I put the flowers there?" Marcy asked, skipping ahead. She knew exactly where she was going.

"Yes, honey, you can." She ran back and took them from Bill's wife, then ran ahead and placed them carefully on the headstone. Once she'd gotten them just as she wanted, she skipped away, running among the headstones, laughing and reading some of them.

Bill stood over the stone he'd had placed there so many years before when her family had turned away from her once again, even in death. Along with her birth and death dates, it simply read:

CLAIRE STEINMETZ MCINNES
YOU WERE LOVED

His wife, Ann, leaned against his arm. "Sometimes I wonder if you loved her more than you love me," she smiled.

"Never wonder that, dear," he said as he kissed her temple. "Go collect little miss Marcy and let's go home."

As she walked away, in a voice too soft and low for her to hear, he murmured, "Never wonder that, dear. I did. And I still do."

ABOUT THE AUTHOR

Deanndra Hall lives in far western Kentucky with her partner of 30+ years and three crazy little dogs. She spent years writing advertising copy, marketing materials, educational texts, and business correspondence, and designing business forms and doing graphics design. After reading a very popular erotic romance book, her partner said, "You can write better than this!" She decided to try her hand at a novel. In the process, she fell in love with her funny, smart, loving, sexy characters and the things they got into, and the novel became a series.

Deanndra enjoys all kinds of music, kayaking, working out at the local gym, reading, and spending time with friends and family, as well as working in the fiber and textile arts. And chocolate's always high on her list of favorite things!

Visit me at: www.deanndrahall.com

Connect with me on my Substance B page: substance-b.com/DeanndraHall.html

Contact me at: DeanndraHall@gmail.com

Join me on Facebook at: facebook.com/deanndra.hall

Catch me on Twitter at: twitter.com/DeanndraHall

Find me blogging at: deanndrahall.blogspot.com

Write to me at:
P.O. Box 3722, Paducah, KY 42002-3722

*Here's a sneak peek
from some of the author's
other titles . . .*

*From Laying a Foundation,
Book 1 in the*
Love Under Construction Series

"I think everything is as ready as we can get it," Nikki told Tony as she stood in the kitchen on that evening, looking around.

"Then I guess I'll lock up and we'll call it a day," He shuffled off to lock the front door. Nikki turned to lock the back door, then turned off the kitchen lights. As she passed the island in the middle of the kitchen, a pair of strong hands grabbed her around the waist and lifted her onto the island.

"Yeesh! You scared the bejesus out . . ." she tried to say, but Tony covered her mouth with his and kissed her – hard. When he pulled back, she was breathless. "Wow, that was . . ." and he gave her a repeat performance, this time running both hands up under her top and peeling it off, then unbuttoning and unzipping her shorts. "You're . . ."

"Determined to have you. Right now. Want it? Say yes, baby," he murmured into her neck, then kissed her again, sucking her lower lip in between his.

"Yesssssss," she moaned, and he dug his fingers into her waist and picked her up. She promptly wrapped her legs around him, her arms clasped around his neck. They made it as far as the dining room table, biting each other's lips, tongues lashing into each other, before he sat her down on it, yanked her shorts off, then peeled off his tee and jeans. He climbed up onto the table with her and stared down at her in the darkness, his eyes intense, almost glowing.

"I should take you right here," he hissed into her ear, then bit her neck. Instead of making it easy for him, Nikki managed to wriggle away from him and took off running, giggling the whole time.

She made it as far as the foyer. Tony caught up with her, grabbed her around the waist, and spun her to look at him. "You're not getting away this time, little girl," he snarled at her. "I've got you and I'm not letting you go." This time, he reached around her and snapped the hooks of her bra loose, then locked his fingers into his boxer briefs, slid them down, and stepped out of them. Nikki purred when she got a glimpse of his cock, hard and waiting. He snatched her lacy hipsters off, then lifted her up again, and she wrapped her long, sculpted legs around his waist.

She wanted to kiss him again, long and slow, but before she could say or do anything, Tony wrapped his hands under her ass, lifted her a little higher, and impaled her on his rigid cock. Nikki stifled a scream as he bored into her pussy and showed no mercy, and Tony groaned and wedged her between his body and the wall, pistoning into her like a four-stroke engine as he held her there. He bit her neck again and, in turn, she bit his shoulder just like she'd done in the back of the SUV earlier in the day. He moaned into her ear, "I just wanna fuck you until I can't fuck you anymore. You are so goddamn sexy that you make me crazy for you."

"Then fuck me," she whispered back. "Fuck me hard. Just pound me until I scream for you to stop."

"Like I'd listen," he snickered and tied into her. His mouth found hers, and he kissed her so hard that she was sure he'd bruised her lips, then he latched onto her neck again and kissed, sucked, and bit it until she was nearly mad. He worked fast and hard, enjoying her cries against his collarbone, the pulses of her hot, wet sheath around his cock, and the hardness of her rigid peaks against his chest. He wished he could stop time or at least pause it, make a mental picture of them together, freeze the intensity of the sparks she gave off as her flint and his stone came together, as one's body burnished the other's to brilliance in that moment, so he could always recall it. Wanting to capture it all so he could enjoy it again later, sit in his office and think about it, picture her in his mind while he was at a jobsite, dream about her as she lay beside him sleeping in the night, he listened to her, soaked in the feel of her skin. He waited as long as he could before he poured himself into her in a gasping, moaning thrust that tuned her up until he was sure that Helene could hear them, even down at her house. Hell yeah, he hoped she could.

His possession of her body was too much for Nikki, and she tightened and came around him, screaming out, her fingers in his hair. When he stopped, she leaned in and locked her lips onto his, holding his face against hers until she couldn't breathe. "Sweet mother of god, babe, what's gotten into you today?" she panted when she finally broke the kiss.

"You. You're under my skin. Permanently. And I'm not complaining – not at all!" he laughed, then kissed her again. "I think it's about time I started living a more spontaneous life, stop planning everything out to the letter, start fucking you when I want, where I want, how I want, and making you want it too. And do you want it?" he asked with a seriousness that startled her.

"Want it? God, I crave it. Just cut loose!" she laughed back and kissed him.

"Let's go finish this in the bedroom," he told her as he carried her up the stairs. "I'll show you 'cut loose!'"

Thirty minutes later, she was still overwhelmed with his pressure inside her, his big, dark hands on her pale skin like molten lava, molded to her, pouring over her, twisting and pulling her nipples, flicking and stroking her clit. The sight of him above her drove her to the edge until his eyes closed and she saw that look on his face that said he was lost in ecstasy, lost in her. That look was all she needed; her own need consumed her and, as he buried himself in her over and over, she rasped her clit against his pelvis and came, repeating his name like a prayer. Within seconds, he groaned out his own climax. The liquid fire of his seed filled her, and she fell onto his chest, panting and moaning. His arms encircled her and tightened against her skin, and she'd never felt so desirable or so loved, so satisfied and so hungry for more.

"Are you trying to kill me?" she asked as he burrowed his face into her hair and kissed the top of her head.

"Yes. Death by sex," he chuckled as she licked his nipple.

"Correction: Death by great sex. Big difference," she giggled as he kissed the top of her head again. "But what a way to go!"

From Tearing Down Walls,
Book 2 in the
Love Under Construction Series

The club was starting to fill up, and the bar was busier than usual. Laura was drawing a couple of beers from a tap when she heard a woman at the bar say, "Holy shit, who's that? That's one extremely tall, dark, and hot Dom. Wonder if he's got a sub?" Laura turned to see who she was talking about and nearly fainted.

It was Vic Cabrizzi. And it was a Vic Cabrizzi she'd never seen before.

The mild-mannered man who'd sidled up to the bar and tried to make small talk with her was nowhere in this guy. Vic was six feet and eight inches of pure, dark, steaming sex in leather. He had the top half of his elbow-length black hair pulled up in a half-tail with a leather wrap, and his torso looked like it was trying to escape through the skin-tight black tee he was wearing. As he made his way toward the bar, the crowd parted to let him through as though they were in awe of the masculinity gliding across the room like a panther. Her eyes couldn't help but be drawn to his ass, and it looked especially fine under those leathers, not to mention the more-than-obvious bulge in the front of them. The room started to get spotty, and Laura realized she'd been holding her breath. *What the fuck?* was all she could get to run through her mind.

"Well! Guess by the look on your face that you approve of our newest service Dom!" Steve walked up to the bar and took a stool. Even in the dim lighting, Steve could see Laura's face turn three shades of red.

"Cabrizzi? Are you kidding?" she asked, incredulous. "You can't be serious!"

"Look at him, Laura. Tell me you don't want that," Steve grinned.

"No. I don't." *Do I?*

"Liar. Have a fun evening. I'll check on you in a bit." Steve walked away and left Laura to stew.

"Hey, can I get a diet soda?" Vic asked as he leaned backward against the bar. Laura hadn't seen him come up, and she jumped about a foot. "Damn, woman, I just want a drink. I'm not gonna slap you or anything. Calm down," he snapped, not even cracking a smile.

"Don't you want your usual beer?" she asked, surprised that he'd asked for a soft drink.

"Nope. Against the rules."

"Whose rules?" Laura asked.

"Mine." She sat the drink in front of him and he picked up the glass. She couldn't help but notice how elegant his hands were, long, strong fingers with just the lightest dusting of dark hair across them. Looking at them made her feel odd. "Can't drink alcohol and keep my wits about me with a sub."

"You're serious about this, aren't you?" Laura asked, her mouth hanging open.

The new Vic Cabrizzi looked into her eyes and asked, "And what would make you think I'm not?" The low growl in his voice made her insides quiver, and she had to look away. "That's exactly what I thought." He finished the drink and smacked the glass onto the bar, then walked away. *What the hell?*, Laura thought. She looked down and saw her hands – they were visibly shaking.

Several of the unattached women in the club spent most of the evening talking to Vic, but most of them wanted to be collared by a Dom – right that minute. And Vic was not interested in that at all. They could flirt all they wanted, but it got them nowhere. He made it clear: He was a service Dom, and he'd be glad to meet their needs, but that was it.

"Oh my god! He's so gorgeous!" one woman was gushing as she and another woman walked up to the bar. "Can I have a Bud Light?" she asked Laura, who pulled it and sat it down in front of her.

"I'd take him on in a New York minute," her friend said. "I needed a sign that said 'slippery when wet' just standing there talking to him!" Laura wanted to throw up.

"I want to climb up there and let him spank me good, but he's so damn big, he's kinda scary," the first one said. *Ha! Wish he could hear that!*, Laura thought.

But that left her wondering why she wanted him to fail. He'd obviously worked hard to train with Alex. She should be happy for him, that he was more confident and looked better, happier, than she'd ever seen him. Why did seeing him looking and feeling good make her feel so bad? *Maybe I'm the bitch that José said I am.*

Laura felt her phone vibrate in her pocket and she pulled it out to see an unfamiliar number on the screen. She'd advertised to try to find a roommate, and she hoped that someone was responding. When she answered the call, a male voice said something, but the club was too loud. "Hang on just a minute, please. I can't hear you." She looked around – no Steve. "Hey, Vic!" she yelled. Vic broke away from a beautiful, bare-breasted brunette and came over to the bar. "Hey, I've got a phone call. Can you watch the bar for just a minute?"

"Yeah, but just a minute. Get your ass right on back here," he said. He'd never talked to her like that before, and she was taken aback, but she didn't have time to worry about that.

Jetting out the side door behind the bar, she put the phone back up to her ear. "Yeah, sorry about that. Can I help you? Are you calling about the ad for a roommate."

"No." Something about the voice made her feel odd. "Laura? Laura Billings?" Her hands went cold and a buzzing started in her ears. "Billings?"

"Who the hell is this?" she growled into the phone.

"Laura, I'm so sorry to call you and drag all of this up. This is Brewster. Please don't hang up on me."

"DON'T CALL ME AGAIN!" Laura screamed into the phone, then hit END and dropped the phone on the ground. It promptly rang again; same number.

She stared at the phone. Everything was coming at her in a rush, and the earth seemed to tilt. She hit ACCEPT and asked through gritted teeth, "What the hell do you want?"

"Laura, please, don't hang up. I need to talk to you. I want to make this right; we all do. Well, almost all of us. I hear a lot of noise in the background. Can I call you later? Or tomorrow? It's important."

"I can't believe you'd have the nerve to call me. How did you find me?" she was whispering, feeling so weak that she could barely speak.

"Billings, I know it's hard to believe, but I want to make this right. It's eaten at me for years, ruined my life and I'm betting yours too, and it's time to man up. Please. Let me do this, me and the others. Please?"

Laura's head was spinning and she felt like she was going to throw up. It was a little late for an apology, but it was more than she'd gotten over the last sixteen years, sixteen years of sheer hell. "Call me tomorrow. Ten o'clock tomorrow morning. That's Eastern Time."

"Okay. Ten o'clock tomorrow morning. Will do." The phone went dead. Laura stood staring at the phone, her hands shaking so hard that she could barely hold it. After a minute or two, she walked back through the side door and up to the bar.

"Where the hell were you?" Vic barked. Then he got a good look at her face. "God, Laura, what's wrong?" She stared at the bar, and Vic grabbed her arms and spun her to look at him. "Talk to me. What is it?"

Laura shook his hands off. "Don't touch me. Leave me alone. Nothing's wrong." She grabbed the towel and started wiping.

She heard Vic say, "That's a lie. I don't believe it for a minute. And when you decide you need someone to talk to about whatever just happened, find me. I can't speak for anyone else, but you can always trust me. I'd never hurt you, not in a million years." Laura turned to apologize to him for the way she'd talked to him, but he was gone.

Vic walked into the men's locker room and leaned against the wall. He knew damn well something had happened, but the ice princess wasn't going to tell him what or take any help from anyone. And he was done with trying to get someone who didn't want to be around him to open up to him. That was a dead-end street, and he'd walked down too many of them already.

From Renovating a Heart,
Book 3 in the
Love Under Construction Series

An hour and fifteen minutes into his Wednesday work day, his phone buzzed. "Steve, your nine thirty appointment is here."

"Yeah, okay, it's . . ."

"Miss Markham?"

Steve wracked his brain – he didn't know a woman named Markham. "Send her on in." He put his jacket and his professional face on, then took his seat behind the big mahogany desk.

The door opened and Angela, Steve's assistant, ushered the woman in. Steve's eyes went wide and a huge smile spread across his face. "Kelly!"

"Hi Steve! Wow, nice office!"

"Thanks! I didn't recognize your last name. Glad to see you! Want something to drink?" She shook her head. "So what can I do for you?" he asked, motioning for her to sit in one of the chairs in front of his desk.

Pinkness spread across her cheeks and her hands shook as she pulled a document out of her purse. "I talked to Nikki. She said you were the person I needed to talk to; she said you'd understand." Steve unfolded the document she passed to him.

It was a submissive's contract. He blinked a couple of times to be certain he was seeing it correctly. Sure enough, the submissive's name was plain on the top of the document: Kelly Markham. Now he understood why Nikki had sent her to him. "This was very well done. Did he break the contract with you?"

"Sort of." Kelly's gaze fell to her hands in her lap. "He passed."

"Oh my god! I'm so sorry! How long ago was this?"

"Nine years." She sniffed. "I still miss him every day."

Steve came around from his desk chair to the armchair next to Kelly. "So how can I help?"

"He made this out thinking it would protect me. Then when he died and we weren't married, his kids took everything, even some of the gifts he'd given me over the years. I'm about the same age as they are, so they saw me as a gold-digger who just wanted him for his money. They even called me a pervert because they didn't understand our lifestyle. I would've married him if he'd ever asked, but he never did. But he loved me, he really did, and I loved him. Even though I could've used the money, I just gave up – it wasn't about money to start with. And I've done okay until Friday when I lost my job. We think they want to close the branch of the insurance company where I worked, and they just laid me off. I've got three months' severance and I'll draw unemployment, but it's not much. I know Dom/sub contracts aren't legally binding, but I was wondering if . . ."

"No, they're not. But this one clearly shows intent. He genuinely thought he'd protected you by making this contract. I wish it had worked." Steve thought for a minute. "You know, I don't want to get your hopes up, but let me see if I can find something, a case precedent or a loophole, anything, that could help. Can I make a copy of this?"

"Sure! Please! How much will you charge me? Because I don't have any . . ."

"You're Nikki's friend, and you took Laura in when she needed a place to hide. Just consider this my way of repaying you."

"Oh, no, I couldn't . . ."

"Oh yes, you can and you will." Steve took the contract out to Angela and asked her to make him a copy. When he came back, he asked Kelly, "Did Nikki by any chance tell you . . ."

"That you're in the lifestyle? Yeah. That's why she told me to come and talk to you."

"Did she tell you that I have a fetish club in Lexington?" *Boy, I'd love to see her in nothing but a smile!*, he thought.

"No! She didn't! I'd love to visit sometime." Kelly's eyes were sparkling now.

"I'd love for you to visit. Just give me a call and let me know you're coming so I can be looking for you. I'd love to show you around."

"I'll do that. And thanks, Steve. I really appreciate this."

"No problem." As she left, he handed her a card for the club with his signature on the back. He was glad she'd come in, and he hoped she'd come by and like the club enough to stick around, because he was itching to see those tits bare. He knew they were fake, but they were real enough for him.

I hope you enjoyed these excerpts from the Love Under Construction Series. *Don't forget to get The Groundbreaking, the free prequel to the series that introduces readers to the main characters in all of the novels. Check your favorite online retailer for the format that works best for you.*

Here's an excerpt from Adventurous Me,
a new novel by author
Deanndra Hall

"Well, don't you look lovely?" Dave says in greeting when I get to the club. "Looks like you went shopping!"

"Yeah! Like it?" I twirl for him in the cute little skirt and the purple bra-thing. The purple shoes look nice with it.

"Yeah, just one problem." He takes me by the elbow and leads me back to the locker room area, then points through the doorway. "Underwear."

"I put on my best ones . . ."

"Not allowed. Take them off. Then come back out to the bar. I'll be waiting." He turns and walks away without another word.

I drag myself into the locker room and pull off my panties. Trying to figure out what to do with them, I put them in my purse and my purse in a locker, and use the combination lock I brought with me to secure it all. When I go back out to the bar, I feel like everyone in the place can tell I don't have on any underwear. Then I realize that the other women most likely aren't wearing any either. At the bar, Dave doesn't say anything. He just motions for me to turn around backward. Once my back is to him, he reaches down and pulls up my skirt, right there at the bar. Before I can protest, he drops it and says, "Better. Now, we need to sit down and go over this training schedule."

His hand grabs mine and he leads me over to a leather sofa. Instead of sitting, I just stand there. Quick as a wink, he says, "Sorry!" and reaches over to a table next to the sofa. There's a stack of towels there, and he drapes one onto the sofa, then motions for me to sit. Problem solved. Apparently that's pretty common around here too. "You need to know that there's really no such thing as 'training' a sub. Each Dom has his own likes and expectations, so they pretty much do their own training once you've got a contract. This is just a manner of introducing you to the lifestyle and letting you become accustomed to the most common things a Dom will expect. That way you can kind of determine if this is really something you want. So here's what I came up with."

We look over the schedule. Apparently under his tutelage I'm going to learn to give oral sex, get oral sex, comply with various types of bondage and discipline, use sensory perception while blindfolded, follow orders, and have anal sex. I will be undergoing orgasm denial, orgasm torture, and various types of deprivation. I have no idea what that means, but I'm sure I'll find out. While we work together, I'm to call him "Sir," and when we're scening together, I'm to call him "Master;" that's easy enough. We will use every piece of equipment in the house, and he'll also be using all kinds of toys on me. That should be interesting. Mattel and Fisher-Price come to mind, but I'm pretty sure they don't make these kinds of toys.

"So at which of these times will we be having sex?" I ask. I want to be prepared.

"For any of these training sessions, if you have a clitoral orgasm, you'll want to have sex. Otherwise, it's at my discretion."

"I'm trusting you to be discreet. Sir." Dave smiles, and I feel better about the whole thing.

"And I'll be training your body to come on command."

"I'll already be there," I say, confused.

"No, come." Then it sinks in and I know what he means.

"On command?" That sounds impossible.

"Yes. You'll hear my voice and you'll immediately get wet. And when I tell you to, you'll come, have an orgasm. It'll take a while, but you'll get there. Then the trick will be to transfer that ability to a Dom when you take one."

"You mean when he takes me, right?"

"Different clubs and Doms do it different ways. Some have the sub offer the collar. We typically have the Dom offer it. There will be a ceremony, and the sub stands and is offered for collaring. If a Dom thinks he can be the one she needs, he'll come forward and offer to collar her. She can choose to accept or decline. If she accepts, he'll offer her his collar. Usually, if the sub thinks he can be the Dom she needs, she'll accept it." Dave smiles. I have to wonder if he ever had a long-term sub.

"But doesn't love have anything to do with it?" It seems to me that it should.

"It doesn't have to, little one. But it's wonderful when it does."

I stop for a second and look into his face. "Dave, why are you doing this? Why would you waste all this time on me?"

He smiles and puts a hand on my cheek. "Any time I spend with you won't be wasted. When I saw you at the bar, I knew you were a born submissive, could just tell. You're a diamond in the rough when it comes to your skills. But I don't think it'll take much to turn you into a sub any Dom would be proud to collar." When a tear forms in my eye, he says, "I don't think you have any idea how special you are."

He's right. I sure don't. And I think he's crazy for thinking that, but I like to hear him say it anyway.

Adventurous Me – available early spring 2014 at all major ebook retailers, and in print!

Connect with Deanndra on Substance B

Substance B is a new platform for independent authors to directly connect with their readers. Please visit Deanndra's Substance B page (substance-b.com/DeanndraHall.html) where you can:

- Sign up for Deanndra's newsletter
- Send a message to Deanndra
- See all platforms where Deanndra's books are sold
- Request autographed eBooks from Deanndra

Visit Substance B today to learn more about your favorite independent authors.

46764992R00170

Made in the USA
Charleston, SC
24 September 2015